# About the

Catherine Yardley was an actor in London for over ten years. She was in a Placebo music video and acted opposite Eddie Marsan in Junkhearts. She also performed in the West End. Her debut novel, *Ember*, came out in 2022. She also wrote *How to Be a Successful Actor: Your Essential Guide to Becoming an Actorpreneur. Where the Light is Hottest* is told from an insider perspective. It gives a unique insight into the acting industry and how it has changed over the years. Most importantly, *Where the Light is Hottest* is a book that shows how beautiful life is when you go after your dreams. Catherine has been featured in *The Guardian, Newsweek, Glamour, Writing Magazine, Writer's Forum* and *Huffpost.*

# Where the Light is Hottest

Catherine Yardley

Where the Light is Hottest

Pegasus

A CIP catalogue record for this title is available from the British Library

ISBN-978-1-80468-068-1

*Pegasus is an imprint of*
*Pegasus Elliot MacKenzie Publishers Ltd.*
www.pegasuspublishers.com

First Published in 2025

**Pegasus**
**Sheraton House Castle Park**
**Cambridge CB3 0AX England**

Printed & Bound in Great Britain

# Dedication

For all those brave enough to go after their dreams.

# Acknowledgements

First and foremost, to my godmother, Margaret Graham, who is always amazing and supportive. You were the first person to read this novel and your words helped me carry on.

To my debut group, strap in, as ever. You have saved me many times. To my querying group, ditto. May the publishing gods shower gold on you all.

# Chapter 1

I stretch out my long legs. They are fake-tanned and honed to perfection. Imogen notices. Of course, she does. I work hard at physical perfection. Imogen finally manages to drag her eyes away and looks into my eyes. She gives me a huge smile.

'So, you must be happy. You have it all now; the Oscar, the husband, the kids. Where could you possibly go next?'

I look at Imogen and smile back. Imogen is one of the good ones. She has always been kind to me. I always take note of the kind ones. You have to remember who is on your side.

'That is a good question. What is next? I guess I have peaked.' I laugh and Imogen does too.

'Well, I'm sure that's not true. Your career has been stratospheric and you always have some other big project on the go.'

I thank Imogen and smile at the compliment. If only, she knew the amount of work it took to get here. My life is a mess at the moment. I am struggling to find another role that suits me and my marriage is falling apart. I am trying to hold everything together, but I am an actor so I act out the role, everyone wants me to play, of the woman with the perfect life.

I wonder how it has come to this. Playing the role of the perfect woman with the perfect life while my real life is really one big, miserable mess.

'I have a few things in the works. I can't really talk about them at this stage.'

*Ah*, that old chestnut. Actors and journalists both know that is code for "I have nothing lined up and my career is on the way down". The acting industry runs on lies. Confessing to failure is for losers only and no one hires them.

What follows is an uncomfortable silence. I can tell Imogen is losing interest. That she is wondering if I am truly worthy of the front cover of Glamorous magazine after all. I do not let the panic show on my face, but it is there.

'What about a tour?' Imogen asks, looking hopeful.

Always eager to keep the press onside, I stand up and gesture with a flourish. 'Follow me!'

Imogen gets up in a graceless way. She is wearing heels and looks like a newly born fawn; she can barely stand in the heels, never mind walk. I fix a smile on my face and pretend not to notice. Imogen must be twenty-five, if that. She seems ambitious, sweet and eager-to-please. I am not sure if she quite has the steel to make it to the top, but she is interviewing me, so she must have something. My guess would be family connections. Or an expensive Oxbridge education.

We go from the living room, down the hall and into the kitchen.

'Wow!' Imogen says. I do not want to think about what kind of accommodation Imogen lives in. It is probably some nasty, tiny room on the fringes of London. I shudder before I can help myself. I could never be poor again. I do not have it in me. Poverty is not for the weak and being rich makes you weak.

Imogen's mouth is open and her eyes are wide. I doubt Imogen is even a millennial. What is the generation after millennials? Z? I can't even remember. I wonder if Imogen thinks that she will ever live somewhere like this, or if she knows it is out of her reach.

'We worked with an architect to do the entire place and then Kelly Hoppen helped us decorate. Kelly has such great taste. The beams are my favourite. I love natural wood. The skylights are wonderful – I just love natural light. The island is an essential when you have a family. You need space to cook.'

Imogen turns to me, an edge to her look.

'Oh, you cook?'

I smile a tight smile. She got me.

'Occasionally.'

I open the bifold doors to my right and the living room and kitchen becomes open-plan.

'We designed it like this so the entire space can be open. It's nice when some people are in the kitchen and others are in the living room. We can all feel like a family.'

'The garden is huge.'

'Yes, it is. The children love it.'

'I saw this place in *Elle Decoration* but seeing it in person is so much better. Let's see the rest.'

We walk on the plush carpet as we make our way up the stairs. I love the feel of this carpet on my feet. It is the most expensive one they had.

I show her the children's room, but I insist that she does not write about them. We go into all the bathrooms and even my bedroom. The walk-in wardrobe makes her eyes almost pop out.

'Wow!' she says for the millionth time. 'Look at all these shoes and clothes. You really have made it. Your life is perfect.'

I smile again, my jaw aching from the effort. I feel proud, and yet a sadness sits there, weighing me down. I am so sick of the superficial. My life may seem peachy but the surface is just as fragile as that fruit. I look at Imogen and give her my biggest smile yet.

'Yes, it is.'

*Then*

'Who do you think you are?'

I look at my brother. I am so sick of this question. All I get from other people is doubt. I told my mother I want to be an actress and in return, she laughed in my face. It had hurt but it helped. I am steel. Pure fucking steel. I was born for greatness. I have known it my entire life. No one will deter me and no one can tell me I am not good enough.

I look at my brother and smile at him, even though I feel as if I am breaking inside. Again, my family never believe in me. They don't even try to pretend. At least it makes me more determined.

'I'm just trying, Liam. I just want to make something of my life.'

Liam looks at me and sneers.

'People like us don't become actors. You will never be rich and famous.'

I leave the living room with its hideous yellow and brown seventies-style wallpaper and worn, brown carpet and close the door behind me. How many times do I have to hear that? It scratches at something deep inside of me. It pokes at my innermost fears. Maybe he is right. The evidence would suggest so but if I do not try then it will never happen anyway.

I am heading to London for an audition. It is freezing and already dark and I have to walk to the train station, get on a train to Glasgow, and then catch a night bus. The entire process takes about ten hours.

The autumn season may be gorgeous but it is gloomy and cold. I get on the train and watch the towns and countryside go by. The train is my favourite mode of transportation but I can't afford to take it all the way to London. I lie all the way back in my seat and think about how beautiful Scotland is. Maybe when I am older, its beauty will be enough to hold me, but not now. My youth yearns for something more.

I board the night bus and I settle into my seat for the long journey. I try not to worry about the future but it is impossible. What if I spent the rest of my life on the council estate where I live now, destined for a life as a young mother or a job that gave me no satisfaction? What if everyone else is right? The thought makes me both terrified and depressed. Inside my head is a cloud of fear and negativity that always hums in the background. What am I doing with my life? Maybe I need to listen to this question and answer it honestly.

I should be at home, happy in my own bed. I would be warm and the family cat, Beauty, would be curled at my feet. Instead, I am on a coach, hurtling down the M6 a little too fast for my liking. The night bus jolts from side to side. I try to get some sleep but the hum of the engine is too loud. Someone three times my size is sitting next to me and the person behind me is snoring.

The audition that awaits me at the end of the four-hundred-and-fifty-mile journey looms over me. Auditions make me nervous and I try not to think about what I am about to put myself through. The audition was last minute and the Megabus ticket had cost fifty pounds return. Not a small sum.

I knew I could ace what I was auditioning for. I had talent and passion, but I wondered how far that would carry me. Surely talent was common? It was the element of luck that took most down. Luck was an elusive thing but life was either kind to you or it was not.

I am feeling tired and a bit car sick so I take my scarf and fold it, then I lay it against the window and pull my hat over my face. Some sleep would make all the difference.

I wake up as the announcement comes over the tannoy. We have arrived in London. I pull my hat off and sit up, opening the curtains as I do. I love watching London go by. It is such a huge and exciting city. I get excited as the coach passes through North London and then makes its way, the city becoming grander.

When you get to the centre, you feel the buzz, and as you get closer to Victoria you see the wealth. This is a magnificent city and I just hoped I was enough for it. I had the feeling that millions of people had been chewed up and spat out by London. I can only hope that I will not be one of them.

Finally, we are at the coach station and everybody starts to get themselves together. I gather my belongings and stand in the aisle, waiting to leave. It is only six a.m. and I am hungry. The first thing I am going to do is head to my usual café, which is only a five-minute walk away.

The wooden bench is as uncomfortable as the coach journey that took the entire night. Thankfully, I do not have to wait long until the assistant comes to get me.

'She is ready for you now.'

I smile and follow her in.

There she is. The only agent that agreed to see me out of all the agents. I had gone through the Casting Guilds website and emailed every single casting director personally. Then I emailed every single agent. Then I had done it again three months later when no one replied. Clearly, Louise liked my tenacity. I could feel her sizing me up when I walked in. Suddenly I felt like I was not enough. I wished I had coloured my roots instead of thinking the inch of dark hair sprouting from my head was cool and edgy. Didn't two-tone die out with the Spice Girls?

'Do you have something ready for me?'

'Yes, I do.'

I had prepared two pieces and a song. I went through all of them, one after the other. Louise tapped her pen the entire time. It was irritating but I did not let it distract me.

After I finish, Louise looks at me for the longest time.

'How old are you?'

'Eighteen.'

She thinks on this.

'Are you sure you want to do this? This is a book of actors in the UK.' Louise stands up and heaves a copy of Spotlight off a shelf. The wood groans in appreciation. 'This is the actress section. You are in competition with all these people and thousands more leave drama school every year. You have no training whatsoever; most of these people have done three years at an accredited drama school. Can you compete with that?' Louise's eyes bore into me. I can tell she wants to deter me from an impossibly hard life. She thinks I have no idea how small my chances are of success.

'Yes, I can,' I reply. I am not lying. There is a fierceness inside of me. There is nothing I cannot take.

'Here is what I am going to do. I am going to put you up for extra work and bit parts and you are going to apply for drama schools. Then when you have trained, I will be your agent, but at the moment you are too green. You have arrogance and, yes, talent, but you need more. This is the most cut-throat industry in the world. The chances of making it are ten per cent at most. What do you think?'

'Yes, I will apply.' I have no idea how I can possibly pay for drama school but I have never let reality affect my dreams before. Now is not the time to start.

'It says here you can do an Australian accent. Let's hear it.'

I am taken aback and momentarily panic. I quickly recover and throw myself into it. I have no idea how I have done.

'That was good,' Kate says. 'Welcome to the agency. Well, kind of.'

Screw the kind of. I have a tentative foot through the door. This is a small step on a long journey but I am on my way. Despite the semantics, I now have a proper agent.

But then I have that all-familiar feeling; pure fear. It is fleeting because I know I have something else. It is not just talent. It is not even just a willingness to work hard and chase opportunity. It is the belief that one day all the rejection will pay off. That if I just keep at it, something, somehow, will give.

After the audition, I step into the London street. The next night bus is at ten thirty tonight. I have an entire day to spend here and the tiredness is kicking in. I do not have a lot of money and no clue where I am going, but it does not matter. It is a sunny day for September and I am happy.

I rummage in my bag to find my A-Z map for some ideas of where I should go. After a moment, it came to me – the British Museum. It is free and it would help kill a few hours. You can't beat a bit of culture.

# Chapter 2

## Now

I watch London go by. It is four in the morning and I am being driven to set. As much as I hate the early mornings, I love seeing London like this. There is hardly anyone here. Just delivery drivers and retail workers. It is a snapshot of London life. Of all life. The quietness calms me.

Today will be full on. Some days I just sit in my trailer. Sure, I tend to do fourteen-hour days but most of that is just faffing about while everyone else sets up the shot. I lift my head up and from side to side until I hear a cracking sound. Training for the action scenes I will take part in today has been full on. I am at my peak fitness now. Exercising two hours a day and expensive meal plans delivered straight to your door does that for you.

It is not the stunts or the running that will be hard, but roving Reggie and his wandering hands. Anytime we have a scene together he is all over me. I spoke to some friends about him and, apparently, he does it to everyone. No one ever complains so I was wondering if I should. But I have worked so hard to get where I am today. The film industry is run by a few, very powerful, people. If they blacklist you, it's all over.

I am not ready for this to be over.

I sip tea that tastes like dishwater as I take in the sights of London at five in the morning. I find the early morning greyness soothing as a new day slowly dawns. London is so calm at this time of day, and yet it never sleeps. I can see a group of Asian tourists taking pictures, as enamoured by the lions of Trafalgar square as I was when I first saw them. I see people in sharp suits on their way to work, and dressed up people who clearly have not been home yet, stumbling around. This city has a buzz that never stops. I do not think I will ever stop loving it. We have filmed most of this movie in New York, but London will always be where my heart it.

The National Portrait Gallery stands in all its greatness. A testament to the creativity of human beings. I wonder if my portrait will be there one day, then I feel embarrassed at my arrogance.

A crowd has gathered as the crew set up the shot, iPhones to the ready. I wonder how many Instagram posts this will equate too. A yawn escapes before I can put my hand to my mouth. I hope no one got a picture of that. There is probably paparazzi nearby too, damn! The tabloids love to print unflattering pictures of actresses, especially ones that are in their thirties and, in their opinion, already ageing.

'Tash, they're ready for you.' The AD assigned to me is a young, attractive brunette called Lara who has the mannerisms of a scared rabbit. She always seems so jumpy. I start to wonder if she is using cocaine to get herself through the long days. Then again, it could be caffeine. I hand her my coat and go hit my mark. The director calls 'Action!'

I run, fake gun in hand, trying to look like a hero. 'And cut!' *Uh, oh.* That 'cut' came too soon. I look over at the director Steph. He has that agitated look on his face that he has down to perfection.

'Tash, any chance of you running slower while still looking fast? We might get more bounce that way.'

Bounce? What the fuck!

'Sure thing, boss.' I do the polite smile I do which is my version of 'fuck you.' I am Scottish by birth but I have learnt the ways of the English.

'Slower but faster, Tash. Honestly, not hard is it?' Alex says to me, joking.

Alex gives me a wink. He is an incredibly hot Australian actor who is down-to-earth and everything the movie industry needs more of. I try to not drool over him. His hotness reminds me of the icicle at home. The one that told me last weekend he did not love me any more. He said I had changed. I think our problem is that he never did.

Alex's eyes crinkle and his impossibly blue eyes twinkle.

Jesus Christ. I might faint into his arms.

'And action!'

Steph, the director, bellows again. I try to go slower while going faster and all the while I try not to think about my breasts bouncing. Sex sells. That is important, nowhere else more so than in the film industry where actors' headshots are passed around and our attractiveness talked about in meetings. I guess I should be happy I am good-looking enough to be cast and yet, I am not.

'And cut!'

'Perfect Tash. You always knock it out of the park. That's lunch, everyone. We'll do scene thirty-nine after.' I hate how happy it makes me that I have pleased him.

I look over at Alex. He is not even slightly sweaty and gives me a sexy eyebrow raise.

'Looks like you bounce right after all.'

We both laugh and head for lunch.

We all have lunch together in a private room in a nearby restaurant. The food is good and I pile up my plate. I get looks from people around me. The woman who plays my mother comes up to me.

'You are never going to eat that. Look at the size of you. You won't manage it.'

I feel anger rise in me. My entire life I have had people make negative comments about my weight. Either I am too fat and I need to lose weight or I am too thin and I am starving myself. I can't win. Why do people always think a woman's body is up for public discussion?

I just stare at her because I can't think of anything nice to say. I know I could get her fired and throw my weight around, but I am not that kind of person, even though I want to be that person at times. Despite everything, I still care what people think. I want to be liked. It is a cord, I do not think, I will ever be able to cut.

I smile at her and turn away. I sit next to Alex and put my coat on the seat next to me. To my horror, the woman sits opposite me. She is staring at me and then the plate, making me feel uncomfortable. I try to ignore her.

'So, did you hear the goss?' Alex says.

'I never know the goss. I need to get in the loop,' I reply.

'Jimmy Donnell was caught with the nanny.'

'You're kidding?' I say. My shock is real. His marriage seemed solid.

'Nope. It's going to hit the papers tomorrow. Apparently, the *National Enquirer* has been up his ass for months now. He had to tell Jennifer last night. It did not go down well obviously, she kicked him out of the house. The marriage is over. Those poor kids.'

'Why do men cheat? It's so stupid. They spend years building something with someone and then they give it all up for one night of passion. Or many nights of passion, but you get my point.'

'Well, women cheat too. Otherwise, who would the men be cheating with?' Alex raises an eyebrow at me while he says this. I have been told off.

'I know women cheat too, but I think you get my point,' I tell him, raising an eyebrow back.

'Did you hear about Ashley Dawson? She is having a baby by surrogate but is pretending she carried it. It is the trend nowadays. Women do not want to ruin their bodies. Who can blame them? Children make you fat.' The woman opposite me adds this exciting bit of gossip but she does it while still giving me a dirty look.

'Really? I have two.'

She looks at me sharply. 'Two what?'

'Children.'

Her mouth opens in an unattractive fish manner. 'You must starve yourself. Look at you.' She looks back at my food. 'You will never manage that.'

I stand up and leave, releasing my anger. I am sick of taking shit all the time. The woman looks triumphant as I walk away.

'See, I told you, you would never manage that!'

I am still hungry but I can't eat my lunch. I feel ill now. She has put me off my food. Alex follows me and puts his hand on my arm.

'Are you okay?'

'Yes, I'm okay. I think people just hate thin women. They pretend to idolise them and think it is fat people that are discriminated against but, trust me, we get our fair share of shit.'

'You shouldn't take it, Tash. You're the star. You have won an Oscar and this film got funded on the back of your name. Tell the producer to get her fired or told off or something. You worked hard for your power. You need to use it.'

'But then people wouldn't like me.'

Alex looks at me with those piercing blue eyes that make millions of women swoon. He is a fine specimen of a man.

'Do you think she likes you? She doesn't. She is jealous and bitter and is taking it out on you. Being liked is overrated. You can't take shit from people all the time so they'll think you are likeable. Don't be a doormat. Being an actor is hard. We take so much shit on the way up that as soon as we have power and are successful we need to say no. We have to exercise that power. Do you understand? You're more than you will ever know and you have to stop allowing people to make you less.'

He is right. I have been a people pleaser my entire life. I think doormat is going a bit far, however.

'I understand,' I tell Alex, but I know I have a lot of work on myself to do.

'Good, now I'm going to get an AD to bring our food and some drinks and bring it to my trailer. Let's get away from the plebs.' He is joking but also not. Sometimes you have to remove yourself from the throngs.

'Now that sounds like a plan.'

We end up having our lunch in Alex's trailer for the duration of the film. I get someone to have a word with the woman but I refuse to have her fired. I do not want to cause suffering to another person. It is hard to get a job as an actor, but it is especially hard for an older woman.

Alex gets the best food sent to us and champagne. We watch sports in his trailer and have a ball. I want to introduce him to William. The ring on my finger makes him out of bounds but I know now that he is always going to be my friend.


*Then*


'What does micro-budget mean?' my mother asks.

'It means they don't pay.'

'Oh.'

My mother had driven me to this audition for a micro-budget short film in Glasgow.

It is for an independent film that is being directed by a Glaswegian film director who, despite being only twenty-two, is already creating waves. It seems that every actress in Scotland, and quite a few from England, are in this one, tiny room.

Like most roles, this one does not pay. It is expenses only, but as the film is not being made by a production company with a budget behind them, I do not mind. I need the credit, the footage and the experience. Anything for my CV.

I am trying to get a showreel together, but I only have a few credits and have not managed to get the footage from any of them. My career seems to be halted by a series of catch-twenty-twos. I need an agent to get jobs but need credits to get an agent. I need credits to get on Spotlight but need Spotlight to get credits. I need footage to get a showreel for TV and film work but need some TV or film work to make a showreel.

It is slowly dawning on me that becoming a successful actor is going to be a lot harder than I have thought and I already felt that it wasn't going to be easy.

I do not know anyone in the industry, nor do I have the standard Received Pronunciation. I certainly do not sound like I should be on the BBC. I am an ordinary girl from the suburbs, but I have talent. I know it and other people see it. I will not let it go to waste.

I wait twenty minutes to audition and then I give it my all. The audition is over in four minutes and I can tell the director does not think I am right for the part. Nothing about me has excited him. I walk back to where my mother is parked and open the door. She beams at me immediately.

'How did it go?' She asks and actually seems excited.

I don't have the heart to disappoint her. 'Fingers crossed,' I reply with a smile.

'Excellent,' my mother says. 'Now let's go and have some lunch.'

The Glaswegian film director did not cast me in the end. I was not even shortlisted. Not that I was surprised. Trying to penetrate his icicle exterior and general apathy had been an insurmountable task. He had barely shown any emotion during the audition at all. The actress that was cast had lots of credits, most of which I had applied for but didn't even get an audition for. The real kicker was when I switched on the TV and saw the same actress in a commercial for a beauty product. A few days later, I saw an interview with her in the local paper.

What does she have that I don't? Sure, she is blonder and taller, but I am just as talented as her.

No, I wouldn't allow myself to be envious, nothing came of it. If you wanted something, you had to get it yourself. Instead, I scoured casting sites for more auditions. It was exhausting and really took it out of me. Finding auditions and applying for them was a part-time job in itself. It took hours every day and didn't pay.

I subscribed to The Stage and kept up on all the latest casting news. I was putting every waking hour into this but things did not seem to be progressing at all. Any other career would reward hard work and talent.

Then it came to me; I could not bypass the hard work. Katy was right, I could not just skip drama school and expect to be treated the same as everyone who had attended. I had to apply to every drama school. I would apply for scholarships and, if that did not work, I would have to work my arse off and save every single penny. This would not be easy but there are no shortcuts. It was time to put in the work. I went straight to the website for RADA and I filled in the application form.

I hear the letterbox go and I race down the stairs. I shuffle the letters in my hand and then my heart skips a beat. It is here. I run back up the stairs to my bedroom and I sit on my bed. I need to be alone for this. Posters of Kate Moss look down on me. *Send me luck, Kate,* I think. I open the letter with hands that are shaking so much I can barely tear the envelope. I have never felt so nervous and excited in my entire life. This is either the start of my life, or the end of it.

The envelope is in pieces by the time I open the letter with hands that feel slippery. Then it is there; the first good thing that has happened in my entire life. I have won a scholarship to the top drama school in the country. It has all started. I am going to be an actress. I run down the stairs and into the living room. My parents turn and look at me, surprised.

'Why are you running down the stair? You sound like a herd of elephants.'

I am trying to speak but I cannot get the words out. I am scared that if I say that I have been accepted into drama school it will stop being real.

My parents just look at me and my father frowns.

'I got into the drama school I applied to.'

My father breaks into a huge smile. My mother smiles too, but it takes longer and it does not reach her eyes.

'I am pleased for you, Natasha, and a little jealous, of course.' She looks pained as she says this. It breaks my heart.

My brother, Liam, walks through the door.

'I got into drama school,' I tell him.

'Wow! That's so cool.'

He gives me a smile and then heads into the kitchen. At least he seemed genuine.

'How are you going to pay for it, Natasha?'

'I got a scholarship, Dad.'

'Well done, then! Wonderful news.'

'Thanks, Dad.'

I try to keep the happy feeling I had when I opened the letter but it has already gone, replaced by a dread that feels like it might crush me. What if I am not good enough? This is all I have ever wanted but now I can feel my fear pulling me back to the safety and security of what I already know.

Maybe I would be happier if I spent my life here, surrounded by my family and people I know. Maybe going to drama school and becoming an actor is a pipe dream. I will never know unless I go for it and I know that, despite my fear, I will never forgive myself unless I do.

I spent the next few months selling everything I own on eBay. I work as many jobs as I can and I save. I try to change my feelings of terror into excitement. That is what fear is, right? Just the unknown scaring you.

I am back in London for the day. I have been offered a ridiculously cheap room in a house share from an actor I met at youth theatre. He wants me to meet everyone and if they like me, I will be the lucky one. The room is only three hundred pounds a month, and it would be easy to pay that every month. I even have enough savings to tide me over for a while.

The house is not exactly in zone one. They told me it is in Ealing, but it is nowhere near The Broadway. I walk around all the different bus stops for ages trying to find which bus I am supposed to take, feeling stress rising in me.

Eventually, I admit defeat and go back into the tube to ask one of the staff. Turns out it is the stop right outside the station. I wait and look around the area. It seems one of the nicer parts of London that I have seen. There is a coffee shop on the corner and a lot of pleasant stores.

It seems to take ages for the bus to arrive and when it does, it is heaving. I take a seat upstairs next to a tall, skinny teenager who is buried in his phone. The bus lurches forwards and I almost sit on him. He does not look up.

The bus ride seems to take ages. It makes me feel exhausted that I will have to do this every time I need to get to the tube station.

The bus finally gets to my stop and I have to say 'excuse me' and push through the mass of people as politely as I can. I look around when I get off. There are rows and rows of terraced houses all painted the same dirty beige colour.

Danny mentioned the house was down a cul-de-sac. I turn left and for once my terrible sense of direction has gone amiss. This is it. I give it the once over. It looks four-bedroomed from the outside. It is an end-of-terrace house that has definitely seen better days. My mother always says you should never go for an end-of-terrace. 'You always get robbed.' I don't have anything to be stolen anyway.

I knock on the door and Danny answers. We were never close but we always liked each other. I was the first one to contact him when he sent a mass text about this room.

'There you are! Just in time. Come in.'

I walk into the house. The hall has a worn, navy carpet and the stairs are to the right. I can see into a kitchen with brown old-fashioned linoleum and a lot of good light. The room looks like it has an amber glow.

I give Danny a hug. He is a great guy and so easy-going.

'Let me give you the tour.'

Danny is hot. All of the girls were after him at youth theatre. Even I would have said yes to him in a heartbeat. He is wearing a tight, grey T-shirt. I try to ignore the feeling in my knickers right now. Making out with your new housemate is not the done thing.

'This is the living room which leads to the dining area.'

The living room walls are painted red, which is a bit much, and the carpet is navy here too. There is a TV and a comfortable-looking sofa. The dining area has a table and six chairs.

We head into the kitchen. It is fifty shades of brown and not exactly clean. There are three large fridges and a cooker. No dishwasher. There is a wicker chair with cushions on it and a long shelf, which has two stools in front of it on the wall as soon as you come in. I look out at the garden. It is paved but big enough. There is a bench there, a shed and some plants.

'This looks amazing. What a wonderful place to live, and the light the kitchen gets is good. I love it.'

'Brilliant! There is a bathroom in there.'

Danny points to a door and I go through. There is a bedroom straight ahead and a bathroom to my left, where everything is pink. It is a complete eyesore. On the windowsill are three mini cacti. Still, beggars can't be choosers. If I do not move in here, I have no idea how I am going to survive living in London.

Danny gives me a nod when I come back out and I follow him up the stairs. There are four bedrooms upstairs and one downstairs. Five people including me. I can only hope that the other three are as nice as Danny.

'There are three bedrooms up here and a cupboard. This room would be yours.'

The smell of dampness hits me as soon as I walk in. The room is an okay size. It has a double bed in it and a wardrobe. It has been painted a pale blue colour, like pictures of the ocean in the Bahamas that I have seen. I can see black mould on one corner of the ceiling. The light is good.

'Wow! It's beautiful. I'll take it.'

I will sleep with the window open. Danny's face brightens.

'That's brilliant. I'm glad it's you, Natasha. You deserve a good, cheap place to live in London. We would need the first month's rent and a deposit today. Would that be possible?'

'Yes.' I reach into my bag and take out an envelope. I hand it to Danny, who counts every note. Bloody cheek!

'This's great. I have to move out on Friday so you can move in early if you want. I'm taking part in a tour and then heading out to LA to try my luck.'

I try to hide my disappointment. I had no idea the room belonged to Danny.

'Yeah, I know quite a few people who are doing that. LA seems to be the place to be.'

'It is, they cast more in a day than we do in a year in the UK. Anyway, there is a bathroom here I forgot to show you.'

We walk into the bathroom. It is white and has mould all around the top of the ceiling. It has a shower in the bath and there is what looks like a hole ten inches away from the sink. The floor has the same brown linoleum as the kitchen. You get what you pay for, I guess. It's okay. It's only temporary. I will not live here forever. As I tell myself this, I will myself to make it true.

# Chapter 3

## Now

I reach up and stretch. I hate to sit too long; it makes me stiff. I stretch my legs out too and I look around the room. This is the pinnacle of my career. James McTeer is here. The most famous actor ever. The actor's actor. He has been in over one hundred films and won multiple Oscars. It makes me feel dizzy that he knows my name.

Then there is Meghan Roberts. The biggest female star in the world right now. She is physically perfect and married to the biggest, and most handsome male star. Her life is perfect. I want it.

Then there are the actors like me. The ones that have had success and are perceived as on the up, so they have a small role in this film. There are no small roles, only small actors, as the saying goes. If only it were true.

We run through the entire script. I love these moments.

After the run through, I walk to my car alongside Meghan. I feel giddy next to her. I can't stop smiling.

'That was a good read-through,' Meghan says.

'It was. I love read-throughs. Just telling stories.'

Meghan looks at me and smiles.

'Me too. That's what it's all about – telling stories.'

This is a moment. I am having a moment with Meghan McQueen. I could die happy right now.

We reach Meghan's car and her driver comes out and opens the door.

'Good afternoon, Mrs McQueen.'

'Good afternoon, Steve. Thank you for getting my door.'

Wow! Polite, famous, gorgeous.

I wave her off. I hope one day I am as amazing as her.

I head towards my door. My driver gets out and does the same. I am embarrassed to realise that I do not know his name.

'Thank you so much.'

'No worries, Mrs Jones.'

I smile at him.

'I am so sorry, I can't remember your name?'

'Fred.'

'Fred, of course. Thank you.'

I get in the car and we head home. I am grateful for the short day. I miss the children. I didn't work for six months after Joseph was born, and then Amelia came along a few years after. I had to go to work two months after having Amelia. I still felt guilty about that, but what was I to do? When you are under contract, that is it. You have to turn up to work when they tell you. There is no flexible working. I took my children to set when I could, hired a nanny, breastfed them in between takes. I have had no sleep for years. My husband, William, helped, of course. He has always been a wonderful father, but he has a proper job, working as a lawyer.

This all stopped when they started school. My children go through periods of time where they are mostly raised by other people. It kills me, but you can't have everything.

I dread to think about what will happen if we end up divorced. It looks like it might end up that way. A part of me does not even care any more. You get to that point where staying together for the kids is worse for them because you hate each other so much.

I look at the people on the London streets as we drive. I love driving through east London. It has so much atmosphere. I love watching the young people and how they dress. Everyone seems brave enough to be themselves. It all seems so accepting. I see a young couple walking down the street holding hands. They are covered in piercings and tattoos. I would guess that they are in their early twenties. They look like they are so in love. I wonder what their lives are like. I wonder how happy they are. There are a billion lives out there, a billion ways to live it. But you only get one.

I walk through the door and I can smell cooking. William cooks a lot. It was one of the things I loved most about him. He was a feeder. He did not just feed you with food though, he filled you up with everything; logic, love, confidence. He was always my north star, the normality I needed in my day.

I walk in and smile at him. He smiles back but it is tentative. These days he always holds something back.

The children's faces light up when they see me, and they run to me. Arms open and hearts too. I breathe in their smell and fill up with happiness.

'Good day?'

'Yes, thank you. The read-through went well. How about you? Have the children been good?'

'Yes, we have, Mummy.' Amelia looks up at me. Her chubby little cheeks and big blue eyes set my heart on fire.

'They were angels. For the most part.'

'Thank you,' I say to him and I really mean it. He has never been at fault as a father and he is as stable as a rock.

In most ways, anyway. We have been arguing a lot recently. I hate it. I just want to get back to the people we used to be when we were first in love. Something is driving us apart at the moment and it terrifies me. He is the only constant support in my life. Everything else is bought and paid for.

I watch William cooking with the children, going through the recipe for the pasta-bake with them step-by-step. Then they start to bake. The children are delighted to help and they both lick the spoon. This moment is perfect. I try to bottle it.

My phone rings and I answer it. It is Clara, my publicist.

'Natasha, where are you?'

Fuck. That does not sound good.

'I'm at home.'

'Is William there?'

'Yes.'

'Can you get away for a moment?'

My blood feels as if it has turned to ice. I try to not jump to conclusions. I can see William looking at me, but I can't read his expression.

'I'll be a minute. I have to take this.'

I head into the garden. The air is a cool, welcome hug.

'Okay, I'm alone now. Go.'

'There is a picture of William in a compromising position.'

I fucking knew it.

'Now, it's not too bad.'

Not too bad? She could not lead with that?

'He's only kissing a woman but she's quite attractive.'

I feel like I have been punched in the gut. Had she needed to add in the 'quite attractive' part? I make a mental note to fire Clara at a more appropriate time.

'It will be in the papers tomorrow.'

I look at my phone. There are no missed calls. I put Clara on speaker and then check my emails. Nothing, no journalists asking for comments. Why not? I guess they all went through Clara but, usually, the ones I have a good relationship with get in contact directly. I sigh, this is such a shit storm. I will never live this down. When you are famous, everything gets added to your biography and thrown in your face endlessly. Journalists ask questions about it years after the facts have been revealed. The worst of them will do it deliberately to rile you. Members of the public will give you their opinions, whether on social media or in person. *It all sucks. FML,* I think. *FML.*

'Natasha.'

It is William. Silhouetted in the door. From husband to traitor. How everything changes so quickly. He can tell from my expression that something is up. Somehow, I refuse to act. It is almost like Clara can feel the tension through the phone.

'Get back to me as quickly as you can with a comment. I'll let you go. I'm here all night. Just let me know if you need me.' Clara hangs up.

I do not break my gaze from William. He looks into the kitchen to check on the children. He takes a calculated risk and comes into the garden.

'Natasha, talk to me. What is it?'

'Who is she?'

'Who?'

'Do not play games with me.'

My phone pings. Clara has sent me the picture. I lift my phone up to William's face. He flinches and then buries his hands in his face.

'That is nothing, Tash.'

'Nothing! Your tongue is down her throat.'

'Look, she kissed me and I did not stop her. I am sorry and I take full responsibility for that, but that is the total of what happened. You are away a lot. Sometimes I get lonely.'

Out of all the things he could have said.

'So, this is my fault?'

'What? No, not at all. I didn't say that.'

'Yes, you did. You said I'm away a lot and you get lonely sometimes. Sometimes? What does that mean?'

'It just means I get lonely.'

The tears roll down my cheeks. This is all of my worst fears. I am about to explode at him but then I see the children with their faces pressed up against the French windows. They look sad that Mummy and Daddy are arguing. I hold it all in. I throw my phone at William. He catches it.

'Give Clara your fucking quote. You know the code to unlock it.'

Then I walk back into the kitchen. I give the children a big smile and stretch out my arms. They run to me and I give them both a big hug.

'Right, let's finish baking this cake. We need something for pudding.'

They squeal with glee and the evening is saved. Natasha Jones. An actress to the end. Always putting on a show.

I do not talk to William for the rest of the evening. We have a polite supper where we both focus on the children and then William takes them for a bath and then bed. While he does that, I have a bath in the en suite.

I light candles and use my best bath oil and bubble bath. I body brush before I get in and put a face mask on. It is all to quell the simmering anger. I have to find strength in calmness and not think about my husband in the arms of another woman. The humiliation burns at me. Everyone in the world will know that my husband cheated on me. That our marriage is a fraud. That I am not enough. I wonder if she is younger. I bet she is. They always are. I put some Maria Callas on Spotify. I could do with the voice of a powerful woman right now. Maria had a lot of tragedy in

41

her life, but she was a goddamn striver – like me; Strong women unite.

There is a knock at the door. Not right now, Satan, not right now. I put my head under the water. Blocking him out. That bastard. I can put this off for a little longer. Make him stew.

When my fingers are wrinkled and I feel sleepy, I get out of the bath, dry off and then moisturise before leaving the bathroom. William is sitting on the bed, staring at the bathroom door. I can tell he has been crying.

'Can we please talk about this, Tash?'

'We did talk about it, remember? You told me it was my fault because I work and travel. You were all alone and vulnerable and needed someone beside you.'

William grimaces. He can see now that he said the worst possible thing. I take joy in his pain and his guilt. I want him to feel an iota of what I feel right now. I have never cheated on William. I am not saying I never wanted to. Everyone gets tempted, but I love him and our family. I would never do anything to jeopardise that.

'You're right. I said an awful thing but I didn't mean it. I promise. I love the fact you have this amazing career. Your ambition is sexy to me and you're away sometimes, but when you're home you're always present. You're a wonderful wife. I promise this was just a silly kiss. I was drunk and she kissed me. It was at the Christmas party. Everyone goes out of their minds a little at those things. There is so much alcohol and mistletoe everywhere. It was a silly, small thing and we were embarrassed about it. I never told you because I was a coward, but I should have.'

I think about what he said and I want to believe it. I could forgive that. To throw him out and ruin the life we have built over a silly kiss? The punishment would not fit the crime, but I cannot shake my suspicion or my fear.

'Natasha, we have been together for thirteen years. We have a wonderful life and two children. That's not to mention how naughty you are on Facetime. There's not a man in the world who would not give everything to have you as their wife. I'm the luckiest man in the world and if you forgive me, I promise I'll never let you down ever again.'

I look at him. His handsome face has those crinkles at the side that send me wild. He gets dimples on his cheeks when he smiles. My entire body is attracted to him like a magnet. In this moment I know that what we have is true love. If he cheated on me, I would take the pain of separating from him. I have that strength in me, but not for this.

'If what you are saying is true then we can work on this, but if it's not, I will kick you out. Do you understand me?'

The biggest smile crosses his face. He gets up and comes to me. My body stiffens. I am not ready to give myself over to him. He lifts my chin and kisses me full on the lips. His love rushes through me. My love for him is boundless. My worry is that he is using this against me.

'Let's go to bed,' he tells me.

'Fine. There is no way I am putting out though.'

He laughs. 'Lady's choice. I just want to have you in my arms.'

We both change into our pyjamas and get into bed. Sometimes I sleep in the nude but I will not do that tonight. We fall asleep in each other's arms but I wake up numerous times during the night, worried about what the papers will say in the morning.

The morning is a clusterfuck as I knew it would be, but the only thing that matters is William's comment.

*I have never and would never cheat on my wife. She is the love of my life. My colleague kissed me on the lips and she has sent her sincerest apologies to myself and my wife. I was drunk and I should have resisted. I apologise profusely for that. We are all hoping to put this episode behind us and carry on with our lives. We thank the press for their kindness at this time.*

I feel happy again. Our marriage is safe, but I keep a note of the name of his colleague and William promises to keep far away from her in the future. All is well in my world again.

# Chapter 4

## Then

I finish my monologue and bow my head. I wait for a beat – I know I have nailed this. I lift my head and Mrs Chisholm has actual tears in her eyes. She applauds and then puts her hands to her chest.

'Do you see, class? That is acting. So truthful, so perfect.'

I can't stop the huge smile that spreads across my face.

I look at my classmates as they applaud, few of them seem happy that I am being praised. I guess I should have expected this. It is a cut-throat environment. The nice ones stab you in the front. My eyes rest on Claudia. She does not even try and smile. Claudia is from 'a good family.' No, scrub that, a famous family. All of her family are in the business apart from her father, who owns a multi-billion-pound hedge fund. She lives in Notting Hill. Of course, she lives in Notting Hill. She is blonde, blue-eyed and is a size eight at most. When she talks, she sounds like she has marbles in her mouth. *Bitch,* I think, and immediately feel guilty. She is probably lovely and I am just projecting my insecurities onto her, and hearing that voice in my head that whispers people like me do not get to become actors.

The loudest applause comes from Michael, who I have a massive crush on. He is from South London and is gorgeous. He has the biggest smile and sweetest eyes I have ever seen. He's beautiful.

I take a cheesy, shallow bow and head back to my seat.

Mrs Chisholm is notoriously hard to please. Maybe, I will make it in this business after all.


I walk to one of my many jobs after a day of studies. I make sandwiches and sell them at a deli just off Oxford Circus. Thanks to its location a lot of actors and directors come in. I smile at everyone and dream of a Lana Turner-style big break.

I have a weekend job showing people how to work computer software too. I either work or study, there is nothing else. It can be exhausting but I don't mind. I am studying acting and living in London. It is everything I ever dreamed of.

I say hello to the deli owner and wash my hands, put on my apron, and spend the next few hours serving customers. I get lost in my work. It can be calming, making sandwich after sandwich.

I hear the bell and look up. It's Claudia. Great.

'Hello, Natasha,' Claudia says. She looked surprised to see me.

'Hi Claudia. How are you?'

'Good. You work here?'

'Yes. One of many jobs.'

'That's cool. I love this place. It's so tucked away and the food is great.'

'Thanks.' I smile at her. Maybe she is not the ice queen I assumed she was. 'What can I get you?'

'Halloumi, mint and cucumber.'

'Cool.'

I make Claudia her sandwich. It is a good choice. I never tried halloumi until I moved to London. It is delicious. Meaty without the meat.

'What time do you get off?'

I look at the clock.

'In half an hour.'

'Cool.'

Claudia looks shy. I can tell she is thinking about something.

'Want to hang out?'

I look up, surprised.

'I mean, only if you want.'

'Sure, I would like that.'

'Great. I'll eat my sandwich here and wait for you.'

I smile, excited that Claudia wants to hang out with me. She is so cool, whereas I wouldn't be thought of as a cool girl.

I come out after my shift and Claudia stands up. We head out of the door together and I feel inadequate. Claudia is wearing head-to-toe designer clothes and has a Mulberry bag. I am wearing trousers that are a cheap, shiny material and a T-shirt from Primark. I am sure I can hear the static coming from my trousers as I walk.

'How are you enjoying drama school?' I ask Claudia.

'Gosh, it's great. I mean, hard. They break you down to build you back up, right?'

I think about that. 'Yeah, I guess they do. It is hard but I love it. I want to dive deep into acting and never come back up.'

Claudia looks at me from the corner of her eye and smiles warily.

'You're good. Probably the best in the class. I think you're the one that is going to make it.'

An uneasiness hits me.

'Aren't we all going to make it?'

Claudia looks amused. Well, more amused than normal. Which says something.

'Oh, you are such a sweet girl. Most of us will not make it. Ninety per cent of us will fail – if not, more. The odds are not in our favour. You, Natasha, you have that "it" thing. The *je ne sais quoi*. Even with your regional accent.'

'It's a Scottish accent.'

Claudia gives me a funny look but does not say anything.

'It's a country, not a region.'

Claudia still looks at me. An impenetrable sphinx.

We walk the next few minutes in silence.

'Why don't we go for tea at Fortnum's? My treat.'

I am excited despite myself. I love Fortnum and Mason. I walk past it every chance I get and I have wasted plenty of hours in there just window shopping. 'Thank you. I would like that.'

We take in the London sights as we walk down Oxford Street and then Regent Street. There are masses of people and we weave our way in and out of them. There are so many shops that I still feel in awe. This must be one of the shopping capitals of the world. You can almost hear the cash machines ringing. I love to walk, but I am surprised that Claudia has not suggested the tube or a taxi. I have not met many people who walk as much as I do.

'So where are you from in Scotland?'

'Just outside Glasgow.'

'What about you? Where are you from?'

Claudia laughs a little laugh.

'I am a Londoner, born and bred. I was born in Chelsea and now I live in Notting Hill. It is way cooler than Chelsea.'

I try not to compare, but I live in a house share with eight other people. It turned out that some of the rooms had couples in. There is mould everywhere and the bathroom upstairs has an actual hole you have to jump over. Paying my rent and bills accounts for eighty per cent of what I earn.

'You are very beautiful,' I blurt out.

Claudia is taken aback but then she thanks me.

'So are you.'

'Oh, thanks,' I reply. But, in truth, her beauty is much more obvious. Obvious is always better. I am more of an acquired taste. Claudia has that *va va voom*.

'You showed me a photo of your boyfriend in stage combat class. What was his name, I forgot?' Claudia asks me.

'Matt,' I tell her. He was a boy from school but we were never serious.

'Yeah, he's cute. You two make a good couple.'

'We broke up.'

'Oh, no! I'm sorry.'

'Don't be, it was my decision. He wanted me to stay in Scotland and settle down.'

'Settle down? We are so young. That's insane.'

'I know. He loved me but he didn't support my career. I'm not going to attach myself to someone who will keep me in nowheresville, Scotland. I want something else.'

I can see Claudia side-eyeing me. What is that? Admiration?

'You're going to be a big star, Natasha. I can feel it. You are talented and you take no shit.'

I smile at Claudia.

'Thank you, Claudia. You will be too.'

Just like that the awkwardness goes. We walk together and I am sure I have made a friend for life.

# Chapter 5

## Now

Alex and I have done thirty interviews today. At least. It feels like more. It is a carousel of the same questions over and over again. We must be somewhere in Dante's circle of hell.

'We need to start a drinking game. Every time you get asked about fashion or make-up we take a shot, and every time I get asked about my fitness routine or whatever actress I am supposedly dating we take another shot.'

'Are you kidding? We would die,' I tell him.

Alex laughs.

'I just wish people would stop asking me about lipstick. It's so boring.'

'I know, and they never care what my favourite colour is,' Alex says. I burst out laughing again. How can he be so gorgeous and so damn funny?

The PR comes in. A serious-looking woman with black hair and tortoise-coloured, thick-framed glasses perched on the tip of her nose.

'There is one more interview and then we will break for lunch.'

'*Hurrah!* Food. I'm starving,' Alex says, delighted. But then, he actually gets to eat proper food. Thousands of calories a day go into that man to keep him looking the way he does. I watched with pure jealousy as he ate a chocolate yesterday. I do not eat sugar, bread, gluten or dairy. My meals are pre-planned and delivered to me. William makes the meals for the children and himself. Maybe when the press whirlwind ends, I will relax my routine a bit, but then the pregnancy rumours will probably start.

The next journalist comes in. A fashionable woman in her forties. She has dyed blonde hair and is wearing high heels. This amuses me. No one wears high heels any more. Not unless they are on the red carpet or doing a photo shoot.

We exchange pleasantries quickly and then she introduces herself as Amanda and jumps right in.

'Natasha, first question for you. I was researching and I was shocked to see that you are Scottish, or you used to be.'

I suppress a snigger. When journalists say they have done their research, usually it means they have been on my Wikipedia page, half of which is bullshit.

'I am Scottish, yes.'

'Hmm.'

I smile. She is obviously trying to get a rise from me. Alex looks at me and I give the slightest nod. I do not need him to fight my battles.

'You have completely lost your accent. I guess you are a secret Scot.'

'Well, I went to drama school and I have lived in England for a long time. My husband is English, and I am not sure how it's a secret, especially as you found out with a quick internet search.'

'Do you think you would have been successful if you hadn't lost your accent?'

'Maybe not. I think things are changing now but there used to be no regional accents on the TV. Everything was very white and middle class.'

Amanda seems impressed by this answer. She is leaning back in her chair, iPad on her lap, studying me like we are on Newsnight and I am the Prime Minister. I think she needs to calm down.

'Do you think you will stop doing nudity now that you have two children?'

*Wow! What a bitch.*

'I guess we will have to see if any more roles call for it.'

Amanda does not repress her sniggers; she just scribbles away on a notepad that is on top of her iPad. I give the PR woman a look. She should be doing her job, keeping me away from bitchy women like this.

The PR woman catches my drift and Amanda is told her time is up. She looks peeved and gives Alex a lustful look.

'It was nice to meet you,' Amanda says, aiming her pleasantry at Alex.

'Indeed,' I reply as I watch her go. Alex takes my hand and gives it a squeeze. I appreciate the gesture but I wish he had not, because electricity shoots all the way up my hand. For the sake of my marriage, I have to ignore my feelings for him.

*Then*

My legs do not feel like they belong to me when I dance. Following the instructions while moving my limbs at the same time is more than my brain can handle. I always go to the back of the class during dance lessons. I can still see myself in the floor-to-ceiling mirror in the dance studio, but I hope that no one else notices me.

All I see in front of me are perfect dancers. They do not have to think about what they are doing; their limbs move easily and with grace. I bite my bottom lip and feel like I might cry.

Mrs Reeves knows I am a terrible dancer. I can see her disapproving look now. She seems to have taken it personally that she cannot fix me.

I try to concentrate more. I find it hard to let myself go. Unless I am in character, of course. I have to focus on being in the moment, on the movements, everything. It exhausts me.

Claudia noticed how terrible a dancer I am. She said I was a good dancer but I had to loosen up a bit. I told her she was observant and that meant she would be a brilliant actress. Claudia is a fantastic dancer and looks amazing in the tight clothes.

Our unlikely friendship had blossomed since our tea together. I find Claudia dazzling.

'You're getting better,' Scarlet says, coming to dance next to me. Scarlet is usually at the front, checking out her perfect form in the mirror. She never gets a step wrong.

More than that, she *flows*. Scarlet is a pretty Northern girl. She is from Liverpool but has already lost her accent to the gods of received pronunciation. Scarlet is tiny – five foot one, I would guess. She has long, shiny dark hair and dazzling green eyes. Her nose is slightly too big for her face but it works on her. It makes her look majestic. It takes her beauty from ordinary to extraordinary.

'Thanks, Scarlet.'

Scarlet is a brilliant dancer. She has studied ballet since she was three. She also speaks numerous languages and plays the piano. It makes me wish my parents had invested in me. All actors wish their parents were the pushy stage school kind, apart from the actual child actors, who always say that it ruined their childhood and their lives. None of the ones I have met seem to be happy.

'We are doing Zumba at the weekend. You should join us. You need to be in shape to be an actress.'

I try to not look offended.

'I mean,' Scarlet continues. 'It's fine if you want to be a character actor but casting directors will not even audition a woman who is over a size ten for a lead role. Think about it. We can all go together.'

'I will. That's great advice, thank you.'

I work through the rest of the routine but as I do I see myself in the mirror. I am a size twelve, but a large size twelve as a woman in a store unkindly told me. My stomach is a bit paunchy, and my thighs a little too big. I try to ignore the creeping sadness that is coming to engulf me but I know it is futile. I can wear a mask but inside I feel as if I am dying.

We finish the routine and I go to get a drink of water.

'Hey, don't get upset. You're gorgeous.'

I smile at Claudia.

'Thanks. She has a point though. It's better to know. I just work and study a lot. My diet hasn't been great.'

'Well, let's go on a health kick together.'

'Yes, that's a great idea.'

I thank Scarlet genuinely because I know that her advice is coming from the right place, no matter how hard it is to hear. There are tens of thousands of actors. Maybe even more. I need every edge I can get.

Just as the class finishes, I see Scarlet again.

'Oh, you should also lose the accent. Otherwise, all you will do is Scottish roles, and there are no Scottish roles.'

Claudia and I stand as we wait backstage. We are too nervous to sit. We walked up Malet Street hand-in-hand. We could barely speak, such was the importance of the day. Now we stand here together. The familiarity of this auditorium has become alien and scary. Every rehearsal has led to this point, yet I worry it has all left my head. The darkness of the wings is comforting, but soon we will step into the bright lights. There is no hiding there. I can barely breathe but it is okay, three years of drama school has given me the tools to do this. I have learnt from the best. I block out the fact that there is everything to play for. Tonight will decide who gets an agent and who does not.

The buzz backstage is ninety per cent fear. I see Claudia tapping her foot. This is how I can tell she is nervous. The rest of her is always cool. She seems so unflappable most of the time. I smile at my friend, and she really has become my friend. We have shared so much together. I have never been able to open up before.

I told Claudia how alien I have felt my entire life, never fitting in anywhere, never belonging. When I told her, she said, 'You belong with me, Tash. You will be my best friend until the end.' It was one of the best moments of my life because I could tell it was not just *luvvie* talk. I love her to her bones.

She puts her hand out and I take it.

'Hey, guys, don't leave me out!'

It's Scarlet.

We launch into a group hug and break into a laugh. I am so happy I could burst. We put our foreheads together and close our eyes, breathing in this moment. Then we head to the wings hand-in-hand, knowing we will never forget this moment.

It is hot underneath the lights. They glow, almost blindingly so. The audience is plunged into darkness. This is it; all or nothing. Three years has led up to this moment. It is do or die. There is everything to play for; an agent, the casting directors in the audience and the applause.

We are telling stories and we love it. In this moment it dawns on me that I have fallen in love with acting. There is nothing else that I want to do with my life. There is only this.

# Chapter 6

## Then

It is my first day on set. My first film. I finally arrive at the location twenty minutes late. No one says anything. I have been going around in circles in east London since six this morning. My stress levels are off the scale and it has rained the entire time. The grey clouds look murderous, not just thunderous. Yet there is a happiness in me that will not concede defeat.

This film may be low-budget but I do not care. We are starting with the love scenes first. I cannot think of anything worse but I do not want to be difficult. I will just go for it. I head to costume. The costume woman looks up when I enter.

'Great, you are here. Can you take your clothes off and then put this robe on? Make-up will be here soon.'

I try to keep the smile on my face.

'I was told there would be no actual nudity.'

'Okay, but these things are still filmed in the nude. We have a thong you can wear. That might be okay, if not we will have to put a merkin on you.'

A merkin. I do not even ask what that is because I do not want to know. The costume lady just stares at me.

'Where can I get changed?'

This is all I can get out. I am just saying words until I can process what is happening. I do not want to take my clothes off. I do not want to be naked. I feel vulnerable and helpless.

'This is the changing room,' she tells me with a mixture of bemusement and incredulity. She must think I have no idea what I am doing. She is right.

I just stand there with the robe in my hands. She is looking at me. I cannot take my clothes off in front of this woman. I can feel myself shaking.

'Where's the bathroom?'

Her lip curls but she does not say anything, pointing outside.

'It's the first door on the left.'

I head to the bathroom. As soon as I get in, I rush to a stall and pull my phone out of my jeans to call Claudia or Scarlet. They will know what to do. I call Claudia first. The phone rings and rings. I try Scarlet next.

'Hello?'

'Scarlet, it's Natasha. I'm on set and they want me to take my clothes off. I don't know what to do.'

'You're an actress, Natasha. You do not have a choice. It is that or fuck off back to Scotland.'

Tears come to my eyes. Is this worth the price? I do not know.

'Look, I have to go but be brave. It will be fine. We all look the same. One naked body looks like another.'

I listen to Scarlet; she has a point. I chose this life. I guess this is the price. What else could I do with my life? Go back to a council estate and work in a factory? I have aimed at this my entire life. I do not know how to do anything else.

I give myself five minutes and I brush my tears away. Then I walk back into that room. I get changed into the thong with my back to the costume lady who lacks boundaries. I feel as if she is looking but I do not know. I put the robe on and I feel naked. Because I am. I am only twenty-one, for God's sake. I know I am a grown up but this feels wrong.

I turn around.

'That wasn't that hard, was it?'

I force a smile. A punch would end my career before it began.

'Okay, let's go to make-up.'

I am about to follow her but then she stops.

'You might want your coat and shoes. It's not that warm out there.'

I put my shoes and coat on and I follow her to make-up. She was right to wonder if the temperature would suit me. Maybe if I had my clothes on it would be fine but summer was definitely turning into autumn.

In make-up, I take off my robe and my entire naked body is painted. I cover my breasts at first but I get so many funny looks and raised eyebrows that I drop my arms. I am truly fallen. I feel tears behind my eyes but I stiffen up, cut myself off from everything. I barely exist right now.

The humiliation of someone painting, and even seeing, my bottom eventually ends. It feels like an eternity. I am allowed to put my robe back on. An AD takes me to my trailer. Even the fact that I have a trailer does not help.

I am trying to hold onto anything positive but it feels as if there is no buffer. I am completely alone.

I wait to be taken to set. I just want this to be over and done with. I do not even reach for the phone in my coat pocket. I am trying to just compose myself and ignore the nausea I feel.

I jump when the door opens.

'They're ready for you.'

I stand up and go with the assistant director. We make it on set, even though my legs feel like jelly.

'I can take your coat and shoes.'

I give the AD, a tall, lanky guy with greasy black hair, my coat and shoes. I can tell he appreciates the outfit costume has given me. I feel cold inside. Like I have been injected with ice. The feeling goes all the way to my stomach, and I feel it cramp.

I watch as the actor, I am doing this scene with, comes onto set. He is older than me and has been in a lot of films and TV shows. I guess I should be glad I am in a film with him.

The director beckons me to come over to him, along with the lead actor.

'Right, we will go through the scene a few times and then we will shoot.'

'I was told there would be no actual nudity.' These words fly out of me and I feel proud of myself. The director and the actor look surprised.

'Yeah, of course. It will be fine.'

His words have not filled me with confidence but he says yes. I start to feel better. I just need to get this bit over and done with.

'I do not like to rehearse sex scenes. I feel it doesn't make them authentic. Can we just try and see how we feel?' the lead actor says.

He directs the last bit at me.

'Okay,' I say.

It is not okay.

We get on the bed together and the cinematographer takes different measurements for the light. I see him give a slight nod to the director.

'Natasha, lose the robe.'

Fuck. I take it off. I am now surrounded by hundreds of men and I am wearing only a tiny piece of fabric that was placed over my most private parts. The thong was 'too visible.' They are all looking at me. Then they notice they are looking at me and they try to look away. Or try to be subtle, should I say. The actor next to me takes his clothes off. He is wearing nothing except some kind of sock over his penis. At least that makes things more equal. I note that no one is staring at him, however.

They finish lining things up and we run through the scene. The older actor touches me, he kisses me, he lies on top of me, my bare breasts are on his chest as he pretends to fuck me. I can feel his penis rub against me.

I detach myself from my body. It is the only thing that will make me survive this.

The heat of the water burns my skin. It feels like it will never get clean. Today was horrendous. The room was packed with people. It is on film now. Forever. I have no idea how I will tell my parents. Everyone will see it. I turn the shower off and I dry myself. Then I crawl into bed. I do not even dry my hair. I stay there for the entire weekend.

*Now*

'Mummy, can I lick the bowl?'

'Of course, you can, darling.'

Amelia looks gleeful and gets to work. She is five years old and the most precious thing. Her eight-year-old brother is playing in the garden. I can see him now, kicking a ball around with his father. I love rare moments like this. Sometimes, I work so much I feel as if I merely peer into my own life.

Amelia has already gone through almost half the bowl.

'Leave some for your brother,' I tell her.

She looks disappointed at first but then I reckon the sugar rush hits her. Sugar is rare in our family. A thing for the weekend or a special occasion, so her tolerance is low.

I put the cookies in the oven and then knock on the window to let William know that lunch is ready. He gives me a weak smile and puts his hand up. 'Five minutes.'

I let out a sigh. He has been off with me since I got home from the press tour. I thought that we had fixed everything after the Claire kissing episode. What I could have done to offend him, heaven knows. I feel as if I am the one that is always in the wrong, but he is the one that kissed a colleague. I forgave that and yet our marriage seems to be going through another rocky patch.

He resents me so much and he does not even realise it. I am surprised I do not leave him but I have to think of the children now. They are more important than me. Yet, I worry that our marriage is over. That we are merely co-parents. I don't want to be in a loveless marriage.

It is funny how love ebbs and flows. When you are young, you think you will be in love every single day. You don't realise how complicated love is, and how hard you have to work to maintain it. The hardest thing is to like your spouse every day. Marriage is so complex.

William and Joseph come in.

'That smells amazing, Mum.'

'Thank you, my darling boy.'

I kiss him on the top of his head and tell him to go and wash his hands. William does the same.

We all sit down for lunch and I can feel William just staring at me. The children finish and leave and it is still there. That look.

'What is it?' I finally snap.

'Is it true?'

'What?'

'Do not what me, Tash.'

'And yet I still have no clue.'

'Alex.'

'Alex?' This befuddles me. But then the gears go.

'Are you fucking him?'

I feel like a wave has crashed into me.

'I have never cheated on you. Never.'

I am hurt, but I hold off on it for a moment. But then William looks like he shrinks. He puts his head into his hands and he cries. It takes my breath away. I have never seen William cry. Ever. I rush to him and put my arms around him. He reciprocates and nuzzles his head into my breasts.

'Oh William. I promise there is nothing between Alex and I. I have never agreed to the principle of DCOS.'

William wipes his eyes and looks at me.

'What is DCOS?'

'Doesn't Count On Set.'

William narrows his eyes but I can tell his sense of humour has returned. A little anyway.

'Is that why things have been so bad between us? You seem to resent me all the time.'

William looks surprised.

'I thought maybe you were getting me back for Claire. They say you spend all your time in his trailer. I guess I have been resenting you. I have seen the way you look at him. I feel I am always at home holding down the fort and you are off with some guy you are in love with.'

'I don't fancy Alex.'

William looks at me and cocks an eyebrow.

'Are you kidding? Even I would.'

I laugh.

'Well, maybe a little. But I would never do anything.'

William looks at me, thinking.

'Promise,' I tell him.

'Good,' he replies and kisses me. A passionate kiss right on the lips. It is beautiful.

'I'm glad you have some time off. It makes me happy when you are unemployed.'

I laugh and smile at him.

'I'm happy to be unemployed at the moment too. I miss you guys.'

We stay there until the children come back. We nuzzle and love each other, happy to be in each other's company. All thoughts of divorce melting away.

# Chapter 7

## Then

It is freezing as I step off the night bus from London. The snow crunches underfoot at the coach station in Glasgow. It is six a.m. I do not know why I always insist on taking the night bus. I guess it feels like a waste spending an entire day on a bus.

I look around for my mum as I wait in line to get my suitcase. My last call with my mother did not go well. She complained that I had forgotten my roots and never came home any more. The truth is I can barely afford my rent never mind the coach fare. I might also get an audition at any moment. This is also the reason why I never go anywhere or do anything. I also never cut or colour my hair. I have to look the same as my headshot, always. It is just one of those little things.

I see her next to her black Ford. She gives me a wave. Hopefully she will be in a good mood today. You never know with her and she does not always take her medication and when she doesn't, she gets a bit difficult. I wave back and force a smile. I guess family is something you put up with because you are bonded by blood.

I watch my mother as I slowly shuffle in the queue. She is shorter than me. Stout even. She is blond too, of course, but neither of us was born that way. We have the same blue eyes. She has put on a lot of weight and her red coat is stretching in the middle. The buttons look like they are having a terrible time. Despite the fact she has not aged as well as she could have due to her love of cigarettes, a glass of wine a day (at least!) and the pills she has to take, I would say she has held up remarkably well. She's beautiful even.

It is my turn to get my suitcase. I grab the green Samsonite. It was a Christmas present from my parents. I head towards the car. Dread fills me a little more with each step.

'Hi, Mum.'

'Well, if it's not the famous actress!'

I smile at her. She might not mean it the way it is coming across.

'I'm so glad you graced us with your presence. Your father didn't think you would stay away at Christmas.'

'I'm not staying away, Mum. I cannot afford to keep going to and fro. I also have to work at my job and I can't get a lot of time off.'

'What job?'

'My various jobs. The sandwich shop, the promo work where I hand stuff out. The job I have in a bar in the evenings. I have to work at least three jobs at a time just to stay afloat in London. It is one of the most expensive cities in the world.'

I am exhausted even having to explain all of this. It is easy for her. She has a part time job in a care home and she loves it because she gets to boss people around and tell people how amazing she is. I have always respected her job but she does not have to look down on everyone else as if they are superficial.

'Well, there's always space for you to work with me at the care home.'

For fuck sake, it is like she read my mind. I roll my eyes for the first time. I can tell they are going to be getting a good workout on this trip.

'Acting is such a hard industry, isn't it, love? I mean, it's exciting when people come up and talk to me when I am in the supermarket and talk about my famous daughter because they have seen you in something. Though, I have to admit, it was embarrassing when you showed everyone your hoo-ha and all the rest in that film. I could not look anyone in the eye for at least a year after that. You may as well have been doing a porno. And your poor dad! I thought he might have a heart attack. You could have warned us. Your poor brother and sister too. They got so much abuse. It was nasty.'

I ignore her and look out the window, burning with shame. I feel like I might pass out. The rest of the drive is mostly completed in silence – she's already struck her blow.

Glasgow fades into the distance and the view becomes fields.

'That's a pretty lake,' I say to my mother.

'It's flooding,' she replies.

It is all we can muster until I see the identical houses of the estate we live on. I feel a suffocation that takes my breath away. Small towns with small minds. I have never been a social person. I only force myself to be one now because I need to network. It is work, that is all, but everyone in this estate knows everything about everyone else. I have no idea how they even manage it. Everyone knows everything about me. I can already feel eyes watching me and ears listening. I miss the anonymity of London already. Give me urban isolation any day.

We are at our three-bedroom house. I say 'ours' but it is owned by the council. Still, my parents tore out the kitchen and replaced it and then redecorated every room too. I have no idea if they were allowed to do that. Or why they bothered with something so temporary. Why fix up a rental property?

The sarcasm starts before I even get into the house. My brother is there in the doorway. Five foot and ten inches of working-class pride and just the tiniest of a working class chip on those broad shoulders. He has mousy hair and brown eyes. He is always on the defensive. Always thinks the world is out to get him. He hates the government and the royal family. He hates anything that he assumes looks down on him. There are only two things to his mindset; them and us.

'Oh look, it's the superstar,' he says in his thick Scottish brogue. My ears have to adjust to the accent. I'm not used to it any more.

My sister turns up beside him. She dyes her hair black and has the same eyes as my brother.

'I didn't recognise you with your clothes on.'

They all laugh. I feel upset. I hate my family. I wish I had never come to celebrate Christmas with them.

'Hey, enough of that. I don't want to be reminded. I'm still traumatised.'

It is my dad. Sure, he saw action in the military but my tits are traumatising? You would think none of them had seen a naked body before. We all look the same, for chrissakes. I take my suitcase out of the boot and barge past them.

'What, not even a hello?' I hear my brother say. He can go and get fucked.

The next day is Christmas and I stay in bed for as long as possible. Occasionally, I hear someone make a comment about my long lie-in but I do not care. I cried last night and then I could barely sleep because I was having one of my anxiety dreams. This trip so far has felt like one big panic attack. I wonder if I will get away with staying in bed all day. I didn't think it would even matter. My hopes are quickly dashed.

'Natasha! Lazy bones! Get out of bed now. What time do you call this?' It is Mr Military himself.

I get out of bed and head downstairs. They all turn as I walk into the living room. They smile at me but I don't smile back. I am not in the mood. Every moment since I got back 'home' has been terrible and I would put the 'home' in quotation marks. This is not my home. I have never felt accepted by my family. They do not seem to get how their constant criticism just made me want to run away from them.

'Merry Christmas!' They all say, pretty much in unison.

'Merry Christmas,' I manage to respond. I head into the kitchen for breakfast, making myself an instant coffee and a bowl of cereal before I sit down with them.

They do not acknowledge me. They are handing out the presents. This is a rare moment of restraint; they usually open them as soon as they get up in the morning.

'Natasha, this pile is yours.' My father points to the presents near where I am sitting. I look at his weathered hand which is wrinkled and full of brown spots, much like his weathered face. He seems so much older now. Or maybe he always looked this old and I did not notice because I saw him every day. It is funny how absence changes your perspective.

'Thanks, Dad.'

I have not always loved my dad. He was far too strict on us when we were growing up. We were children, not soldiers, but as I have grown older, I have acquired a grudging respect for him. He has instilled a discipline in us along with a work ethic. I love him too, of course. I love all of my family. Just mostly from a distance.

'My presents for you all are under there.'

I open my first present from my parents. It is a book on how to become a successful actor, which makes me feel happy. My parents thought my career choice was a pipe dream, and my father wished I had done something more serious with my life. To him acting was an unstable career choice, but their shock at my success has sat side-by-side with a newfound respect.

'Thank you, I love it. It will be very helpful.'

The rest of the presents are cellulite cream from my mum (I mean, really!), the hair wand I wanted from my parents, a bubble bath set from my brother, and a DVD of a Matthew McConaughey film from my sister (second hand and with the cheap price tag still on.)

They open what I got them. A smart blue shirt for my brother, a good make-up kit for my sister, a pampering set for my mother and a Wilbur Smith book for my dad. I like to think the presents were all thought out and bought with love. Only my dad looks grateful, even though none of these were cheap. I guess I am always a disappointment to them. I feel like I can never do anything right.

'Thank you, Natasha, I love it,' my dad says, making me happy.

'Well, you could have bought us all iPads!' My brother says. I look at him and try to quell my feelings. What world does he live in? What an arsehole!

'What can I say? Only an idiot would go into acting for the money.'

This is what it always is. A room filled with an underlying tension. Resentment always simmering just below the surface. They seem to hate me because I wanted something different for my life. It is like they think I rejected them, but I never did. I would never judge anyone else's life choices. Why can they not respect mine? I wish my relationship with them was something else but I do not know how to make it so.

Christmas lunch has more cheer. My mother sure can cook. We gorge ourselves on the turkey with the best gravy I have ever tasted, cranberry sauce, honey roasted parsnips, Brussels sprouts and roast potatoes. We have a prawn cocktail to start and yule log to finish it off. I must be a stone heavier by now. I do not want to think about the two-hour daily workout I will have to take part in to get back into shape. All from one trip to see my family.

After lunch, we sit around and play board games and watch Christmas films. We can barely move we are so stuffed. My ribs actually ache. I start to feel sleepy. I could do with a nap right now.

'Hey, Natasha, do you remember the cat we had that used to jump in the bath?' my brother asks. We all start to laugh.

'Oh yeah, Tommy the cat. He loved the bath. He was such a weird cat. I miss him so much.'

'So do I,' my mother says, looking emotional. She cried the most when he died. I place my hand on my mother's back and rub it. She looks at me and mouths 'Thank you.'

For the rest of lunch, we laugh and talk, sharing our stories and I start to feel happy in the warm glow of shared memories and love. We go for a late-afternoon walk and then spend the rest of the day watching TV. Despite everything, I enjoy myself.

*Now*

Christmas in Gstaad – I am not sure, there is anything more beautiful. Everything from the Christmas tree to the lights on the chalets are just perfect. I love this place. It is packed with interesting people. Of course, Christmas is only the warm up. The real celebration in Gstaad is New Year. It is unmissable and awash with caviar and champagne. This little Alpine town is the place to be.

This is William and the children's favourite time of year. We fly in on a chartered flight that I rent through the app on my phone, then we just spend time together, socialise, eat, drink and be merry. The parties are something else. Usually, I worry about spoiling the children, but not during Christmas in Gstaad. I am glad they get to experience this level of decadence. My children are the elite. That always makes me proud. They have been given the best possible start in life. I just hope they run with it. I will be furious if they do not make something of their lives after growing up with such privilege.

The children have been skiing since they were toddlers. They are much better at it than me. I had my first lesson in my twenties. It was always on my acting CV of course. You say yes and then you find a way. A quick speedy lesson means it was never a lie.

We always stay at the Palace Hotel. I do not know how I would cope if I did not have Gstaad every year. Everyone needs to decompress and I live life at one hundred miles per hour.

The children gorged themselves on the food at the restaurant, and we carried them home while they slept in our arms. I love the sound of the snow crunching underneath my feet. The sensation of it relaxes me.

I looked over at William, my tall, handsome husband, as he carried our son and I fell in love with him all over again. His smile is a mile wide. I make a mental note to call my family after we have another glass of champagne and then William and I need to have some time together while the children are asleep. An opportunity is an opportunity.

One glass becomes another and we end up having amazing sex and then falling asleep in each other's arms. In the morning, I feel guilty that I forgot to call my family, but, hey, they did not call me either.

# Chapter 8

## Then

'I cannot believe you are an actual actress now. I am so happy for you, and a teeny bit jealous too.'

I recoil. I hate people who tell you they are jealous of you. It ruins the moment and is so egotistical.

'Thank you, Scarlet,' I say as I sit up in my bed and look out of the window.

Scarlet does a weird laugh on the other end of the line.

'Thank you? Is that it? You got an agent after the end-of-year show and a part in a film not long after. You don't even sound happy.'

It winds me up that she is not even trying to keep the edge out of her voice.

'I am happy, Scarlet. There is no need to have a go.'

'I am not having a go, you should just be more grateful. It has come so easy to you so quickly. It is weird that you sound sad every time I call you.'

I am sick of people telling me to be grateful all the time. Sure, it was luck that I got cast in a film, but it came at a price. I have been to more auditions than I can count. I have worked for this.

'Maybe you could talk to your agent for me? I asked Claudia but you know what she is like. Always a bit aloof, that one. I am not sure she will come through for me.'

'Sure. I will do.'

'I cannot wait until the film comes out on DVD. I am going to buy a copy.'

'Me neither,' I lie. When the film comes out on DVD, I will have to go and live under a rock.

'Okay, bye. Do try to cheer up, Tash. You are so depressed all the time at the moment. It is not normal. You are living the life. Be grateful, for God's sake. Bye.'

And with that Scarlet hangs up. I could not be more happy. I call Claudia. She answers on the first ring.

'Hey, movie superstar. How are things going?'

I burst out crying.

'Oh my God, Tash. What is it?'

I can't speak. I just let everything out. It feels like this will never stop.

'Hold on, I'm coming over. Give me any sound at all if you're at home.'

'Yes,' I manage to say.

Claudia hangs up but I know she is coming and that finally I will be able to talk to someone who will not just tell me to shut up and be grateful.


*Then*


'Just fill in the form and then come back for a picture. There are pens over there.'

The receptionist is the typical London receptionist; posh, twenty-something with hair that is expensive; in this case, highlighted with honey-coloured hues. She is probably also an actor. Or, less likely, an aspiring casting director. She takes a Polaroid picture of me and gives me some forms to fill in, then I walk into a room of people who look just like me. They are my height and around my weight. They have the same eye and hair colour. They all even have the same accent.

Occasionally it got to me, this sense of how insignificant my life really is. How there are so many others just like me. But it is fleeting because I know I have something else. It is not just talent. It is not even just a willingness to work hard and chase opportunity. It is the belief that one day all the rejection will pay off. That if I just keep at it, something, somehow, will give. I had one film under my belt, why not more?

I hand the form back and then I go through my lines, but I did not have to wait long until the casting assistant calls my name. I smile and stand up.

'We're ready for you,' the casting assistant, a bubbly brunette with a mega-watt smile tells me.

I follow her into the room. There are another two people there, the camera operator and the casting director, Greg. Greg is known by every actor in the business. He casts most of the commercials and a good amount of television too. I am desperate to impress him. So desperate, in fact, that I can feel the nerves in every part of my body.

I have to pull myself together. I look down to hide my throat as I swallow the build-up of saliva in my mouth.

When I look back up, I give him my biggest smile and concentrate on the matter at hand.

'On the X to mark your ident. Name, age and agent to camera. After that, you can go straight into the scene.'

Greg is polite and kind. I step onto the X, move ever so slightly to where the light is hottest and then I begin.

'Natasha Jones, twenty-two. Agent is Wilson & Lewis.'

Do the nerves show? Can they tell how desperate I am? I hope not. I get on with the audition. We go through the scene a few different times. I am auditioning to play a kick-ass secret agent in a movie that is filming in London and America. I cannot even imagine going to America. It is the dream.

We do one scene and then I pull my hair back and put a blazer on. Greg looks impressed and thanks me for doing so. We do the other scene. My American accent has been perfected with a ton of practice and an accent coach. I emptied out my savings for the coach. I haven't been paid for the film I did yet so money is low.

'Thank you, Natasha. That was perfect.'

I smile. Perfect.

'Thank you, Greg.' I look at the casting assistant and give her a smile and a nod then I walk out. I feel positive. I really want this part. I say goodbye to the receptionist and cross my fingers as I walk out into the London streets and, even though, I can barely afford it, I head to Fortnum's. I walk all the way. I feel the hot buzz coming from Piccadilly. I see people on the Shaftesbury Memorial fountain, like they always are. The bright Piccadilly lights are loud and brash and I love them. I take in London life as I walk, loving the little pockets that are so different; an entire world in one city. I walk past the huge, glorious Waterstones and I make a note to go in after and buy a book.

I feel lucky to live here, even though I can barely afford it. For the first time since I made that shitty film, I feel happy.

*Now*

'I have to say, Natasha, this is huge. Everyone who is anyone has a franchise these days. This could be your one. They seemed really keen.'

I sip my green tea at our kitchen island and I listen to Louise and I try to not get too excited. The work has really dried up in the last six months and, while I love being at home, I am panicking now. We have a massive mortgage and the children go to private schools. Add in my agent, my publicist, my stylist and the rest of our outgoings and it is a colossal amount. So colossal that William's lawyer salary merely makes a dent in it.

Shit. I want this too much. That is the problem with desperation, people can always smell it.

'You would be filming in LA for three months of the year. I think they'll start with a trilogy.'

LA. I love LA. It is my spirit home. I allow myself to get excited and then I worry about being separated from the children for such a huge amount of time. I put that thought away.

'That sounds great. What do they want from me?'

'Well, they liked your self-tape so now they want a meeting. I will send you the time and place.'

I scribble down the details.

'Thank you, Louise. You always get the best stuff.'

We say goodbye and I hang up. I want this so I decide that it is mine.

On the day of the meeting, I change a million times. The bed is covered in clothes. The floor has become a floordrobe. I have pulled out all my shoes. I look in the full-length mirror at the latest option; a blue satin shirt and black trousers. I think about the email Louise sent along with the details. 'Dress sexy, you need to show your figure.'

I am a thirty-one-year-old woman and I am still dressing for the patriarchy. Will it ever end? When I am old, I suppose. When they toss me out to pasture. It is actually a happy thought. I think about wearing a skirt but I do not want to be obvious. Then I think about the amount of time I have spent in the gym, ditto on the personal trainer. Fuck it, let's go for obvious. I need to sell this.

My skirt is above the knee and the tight cable-knit blush pink jumper suggests innocent but fundamentally is not. I am meeting the director at The Ivy, which makes me happy. As a rule, I keep away from hotel rooms. I have heard too many stories. Hell, I even have a few of my own. I am not adding to that.

I do not need to announce myself to the staff. They know who I am and they know where I sit. The waiter takes me to the table. George is already there. He stands up and puts out his hand. I shake it and give him a smile.

'Hello.'

'Hello,' I reply.

I thank the waiter.

'It's nice to finally meet you. I've been following your career for years.'

I blush. I had no idea.

'Thank you. I have been following your career too. I love your films.'

'So, what struck you about the character? What makes you feel like you're the one to play this badass superhero?'

Oh, wow! He is jumping right in. I take a moment to think about my answer. I can see his eyes narrow; he does not want hesitation.

'I think we have the same soul.'

Jeez, did I just say that? His eyes brighten so the cheesy answer seemed to work.

'She's this tough person with an emotional soft side. She has a higher purpose too; she wants to achieve things that will change the world for the good.'

I can see George thinking about this.

'You're right. I never thought about it like that. She has a higher purpose but a gentle soul. Tough but soft.'

George strokes his considerable beard as he thinks.

'I was born to play this role. We are the same person.'

Thank you, Natasha. We'll be in touch.'

With that, he stands up and leaves. *Just like that. Okay,* I think. That was short and sweet and a little bit rude. The waiter comes over with a menu and my usual drink; a gin and tonic. The G&Ts are perfect here. You'd think they are all equal, but no.

I take my drink and smile. I send Claudia a text.

'I am at the Ivy. Come and join me now.'

She texts back immediately that she is on her way. I smile and take a sip of my drink. I have no idea how that went but I may as well enjoy a nice lunch while I am here.

Claudia arrives in record time. She is dressed head-to-toe in Chanel. It ages her. Her blonde hair is in a messy top knot. She wears a pink lip gloss, mascara and a good foundation. Claudia is the expert at lazy perfection. She always looks as if she should be on the cover of *Tatler* but she doesn't seem to make any effort, nor does she care what you think.

'What are you smiling at?'

'I am just happy to see my friend. You look great.'

I stand up to hug her. I tighten the squeeze and she makes a little noise of protest.

'What are you doing here, and without the ball and chains?'

'I was meeting the director of Women of the Galaxy. That female superhero story the studio is doing.'

Claudia's mouth drops.

'Dude, good for you getting an audition for that. I can't even get an audition for a sanitary protection advert at the moment. I think my career is dead.'

'Your career is not dead.'

'Thirty is death.'

'Thirty is not death.'

Claudia looks at me and cocks an eyebrow. I stand firm.

'Forty is death.'

Claudia thinks about this as I signal the waiter to get another G&T.

'Okay, I will give you that. Forty is death. Nine more years!'

I laugh. A sense of humour is the only way to survive as an actress. The waiter brings Claudia her gin and tonic.

'Oh, thanks, babe. You must have read my mind.'

She gives him a wink and he actually winks back. Claudia is sex on legs.

'So how did it go?'

'I don't know. I thought it was going well but it was short. He left within five minutes. He seemed impressed before he left though.'

'You would be great in that film.'

'I would,' I think wistfully.

'What else have you auditioned for lately?'

'I auditioned for Adam Lowe.'

'Wow! How did that go?'

'It's hard to tell. He grunted his way through it and showed no facial expressions whatsoever. I hope he's like that with everyone.'

'Oh, darling! It doesn't matter. I heard he is meticulous to work with. He spends months doing the same scene over and over again. If he was not one of the old masters then no one would give him money to make a film.'

'I know. I've watched his films since I was a kid and it would make my life complete to be in one.'

I can feel a sadness creeping in. I close my eyes and will it away.

'Let's order some lunch. On me.'

Claudia opens the menu. 'No, I insist on paying. You got the last two, remember?'

I smile at Claudia. She is my oldest and dearest friend. She has never taken advantage of me and never would. We order an eggs benedict for me and a cheese omelette for Claudia.

'I saw A Fair Road again last night.'

I groan. It was my first film. I have blocked out the awful day I did that nude scene. I have learnt over the years to be able to talk about things as if they did not happen to me. I completely remove myself from all of the crappy things. It is for the best.

'They promised they would not show my breasts. They promised no nudity at all.' I try to keep the bitterness out of my voice.

'Oh, darling, your tits looked amazing. So did your arse. Seriously, it has been a while since I saw you naked but I doubt your nipples still line up like that after two kids.'

I choke on some of my drink. Claudia is hilarious.

I think about my body and the work it took to shift the baby weight.

'It hurt a lot at the time. My family took it badly too, but I'm okay now. It doesn't matter. Why are breasts so sexualised anyway? They're for feeding babies.'

Claudia pulls a face. Her mother is French. She spends every summer holiday wearing bikini bottoms and nothing else. The uptight British attitude to nudity means nothing to her.

'You seem to be doing less of them.'

'That was the only time I did my own nudity actually. After that, I always used a body double. I felt guilty about it. Some poor woman having to take her clothes off. When you use a body double, they tend to go to town and the scenes are so graphic. I also have some power now. A teeny tiny amount, but, still. And you have to choose the woman yourself. They have loads of pictures of women who are completely naked front and back, but they do not show their faces. It's horrendous. It makes me feel like a pervert.'

Claudia pulls a face. 'I would rather get my own tits out. A body is a body. Anyway, don't feel bad. You deserve it. You earned it.'

Claudia means this. Claudia is never jealous or bitter. Claudia is my favourite person in the entire world, barring my children and husband, of course.

'Anyway, better her than you. You know what they say, if it's between you or them, send flowers.' Claudia laughs a big laugh and I cannot help but join in. 'You're going to get one of those parts and you're going to nail it.'

'What about you? How are things going? That play sounded exciting.'

'I'm doing the play.'

An involuntary squeal comes out of me. Much too loud for The Ivy. I can feel eyes on me, but then, there already were. Privacy is what you give up for success. At least here they try to be subtle.

'I'm coming to see you every night.'

Claudia pulls another face. Her face is so expressive. There is no reason why I am more successful than her. She even has family connections. It got her in the door and her career went well for a while, but in the past few years it has plateaued. It is not fair but, then again, our industry is not.

'We should do something together.'

Claudia looks excited.

'I would love that. I hope it happens one day.'

We eat our lunch and have more drinks. I have no idea if I will become a superhero or work with the Old Master but I know I will always have Claudia.

# Chapter 9

## Then

I walk to Starbucks. My thighs seem to be wobbling. I need to cut down on my sugar intake. I have still not lost all that weight Scarlet suggested that I do. I hope she does not notice today and, even though I hope, I know she will. Scarlet is scarily observant.

I have started doing the Tracey Anderson Method. It takes two hours a day. One hour of cardio and the other of toning. I am getting better at dance. I can barely do it in the tiny room I rent in that mouldy house.

I have a sofa bed in it and a small set of drawers. The blinds keep falling so I do not open them any more. When I have money, I will buy some new ones. It is not ideal, but anything that means I can afford to live in London is worth putting up with, shitty housemates and all. Just for once I would like to come home and not have dirty dishes everywhere. People never clean or tidy after themselves. They have parties all the time, with their crap music and a carousel of people coming in and out.

I walk in and I see Scarlet is already there. She has been on tour doing rep in schools around Britain. She hates it. I have text messages galore to prove it. Scarlet is ordering breakfast and she looks briefly irritated before she breaks into a smile – she had obviously meant to have breakfast before I arrived. She points at the table she was sitting at.

'What do you want?' Scarlet asks.

'I'll have a tea, thank you.'

I watch Scarlet as she finishes ordering. She is pretty. She is five years older than me. She was a mature student, as they call it. She still looks like she is in her early twenties. She has a very unique face that makes her look even prettier. Her nose is straight and long and her cheekbones are prominent. She got rid of her northern accent ages ago and, thanks to her pale skin, has been cast in some typical English Rose roles. I am also pale but do not mind having friends in the same niche as me. I love acting but a role is not worth losing a friend over.

Scarlet comes over with the tea, making a double journey to also grab her toastie. The toastie smells like heaven and I realise just how hungry I am. All I can afford is one pot of tea. I have already spent the money I made this month trying to progress my career. I feel poor and it brings a creeping sadness that I cannot shake off. I put a smile on my face, hoping it will hide my melancholy from Scarlet.

'How's your uncle?' I ask to cover the silence and take my mind off my hunger.

'As negative as ever. LA didn't work out for him. He went to loads of meetings and nothing came of it. He is in Death of a Salesman at The Garrick at the moment and just moans about it. He hates doing theatre. He keeps telling me not to become an actor. "It's too hard. You never know if you will work again, the pay is awful. I do this shit play every night. The same thing every night. It's bloody tedious and monotonous," he keeps saying.'

Scarlet and I look at each other. A moment of dread passes between us.

'I saw him in a repeat of The Inspector. He's really good,' I tell Scarlet, trying to think of something positive to lighten the mood.

Scarlet laughs. 'He hates that show. He always bitched about how little he was paid and how much he hated the director. God, he's such a grump. Talking of LA. Guess what?'

'What?' I say.

'I'm going to LA!'

My mouth drops before I can stop it. Scarlet has not mentioned LA before.

'Wow! That's amazing. When are you going?'

'In three months. I got a visa. I can't believe it. I had a very good lawyer. Sorry, I didn't tell you about it before. I didn't want to jinx it.'

'That's okay, I'm happy for you. What's the plan?' I ask her.

'I have some friends out there who will put me up. I have an agent interested and I just passed my driving test. It's all go. If you come out, you can stay with me. We can take on the world together.'

I smile at Scarlet, she is such a go-getter. A striver as my mother would call her. I have no doubt in my mind that she will succeed in life. I still remember the advice she gave me when we were at drama school together.

After getting rid of my Scottish accent, as she suggested, I changed my nationality to British. It helped a lot. Even losing most of the weight has helped. She gives great advice and is generous with it. Not all actors are like that. *Schadenfreude* is common in our industry, the success of your friends is not something everyone celebrates. When you do find those people who pull others up, and are supportive, you hold on to them tightly.

'I would love to do that. I've been telling my parents for years that I was going to go to LA. I just want more credits and to pass my driving test first.'

I take a long, slow sip of my tea and try to make it last.

'Well, you have plenty of time. My great plan is to take all the roles of the women who drop out to have babies. The older you get, the less competition there is.' Scarlet smiles.

'That's a good idea. If I have kids, I hope I will still be able to act, though. That would be depressing, to have to give it all up.'

'Yeah, it would. So many actresses end up doing that though. Some come back later but not many. It can really suck being a woman.'

'Well, we are still young. We have a good amount of time yet,' I reply but, inside me, there is a sinking feeling. I am not sure I can fit all of my living into one life.

# Chapter 10

## Now

I want to die. Right now. Take me away from this pain. I hold it for another thirty seconds while my personal trainer yells at me. At last, the longest thirty seconds ever ends and I put down my leg. I turn to look at Joe. He doesn't say anything. He does not need to. His disapproval radiates from him. He waits a beat and then tells me to lift the other leg. Christ. Staying in shape is not for sissies. How can this much torture make you live longer? It is a conundrum.

The forty-five-minute workout finally ends and I get that high I always get. The high is like when you have just given birth and, suddenly, all the pain is worth it. I feel stronger and like I achieved something. I am still holding out hope for that superhero role, so I get put through my paces by Joe six days a week. I am not on my delivered meals because William has started cooking more. He has become obsessed with trying different cuisines. He tends to throw himself wholeheartedly into a hobby, exhausts it, and then moves on. I hope he sticks with this one.

I am going to a premiere tonight with William. I shower after I am done with Joe and I skip home thinking about it. I love it when it is only the two of us.

The house smells clean when I walk in. Ah.

'Hello, movie star!'

It is my mother-in-law, Brenda. She always greets me like that. I have never met a more positive woman in my entire life. She looks after the children anytime and always cleans the house when she comes over. I love her.

'Hello, Brenda.'

I go and give her a bear hug and kiss her. The children see me and run to me.

'Mama, Mama!'

I kneel and they run into me, knocking me over. You would think I was gone for days rather than hours. But I guess they never know. The thought stabs at me, the guilt of being a working mother.

'You see that, it's because you're such a good mother. That's why they love you so much.'

I smile back at Brenda. I got lucky with my mother-in-law. I see William in the doorway, smiling. Suddenly the superhero movie does not matter any more. The only place I want to be is here.

'Something smells great,' I tell William.

'I made a roast.'

I smile. I love roasts. I lift the children, one in each arm. William hates it when I do this. He worries about my back. Husbands never realise how strong their wives are. I kiss William on the cheek and then put the children down.

'I'll just get changed and come back down.'

The children go back into the huge boxes they have been playing in all week. What is it with children and cats? You give them a box and they are happy for hours.

I run up the stairs and I take out my phone to make a quick call to my agent.

'Hi, Louise.'

'I was just about to call you!'

'Oh, you were? That's great! I just wanted to let you know that I would prefer to work in the UK from now on. Maybe I could do some television. The stuff out there at the moment is brilliant.'

'Well, then this will make you happy! You got the part in A Long Road.'

My jaw drops. I will be working with the Old Master. I thought the audition had been awful. I cannot say anything. I am in shock. You hope you will get every job you go for but there is always this sense of disbelief when it happens. Even now. This is one of those moments, no amount of pinching myself will make this feel real.

I walk down the stairs in a daze. William looks at me, concern knitting itself onto his brows.

'What is it, you okay? You look' – he pauses and tries to find the right word – 'pale.'

'I got the part in A Long Road.'

'What?' William asks. My voice is barely audible.

'I got the part.'

Brenda jumps up. 'Which one, dear? Which one?'

'A Long Road.'

William's face turns to pure elation, he jumps up and punches the air. Brenda does this happy dance, which looks a bit like a *cha cha cha*. The children jump up and down too. The entire room is full of happiness and joy. I start to cry and the children stop, confused.

'Why is Mummy crying, Daddy?' Amelia asks.

'These are happy tears, Amelia. Mummy is crying because she's happy.'

William has taken me into his arms and he presses his cheek to mine.

'Well done. You deserve it.'

I try to take in every single moment of this. These rare moments when our dreams come true.

'Right, let's open a bottle of champagne! We need to celebrate this.'

Brenda knows we always keep a bottle in the fridge. She is already popping the cork. Sunday lunch is about to become very boozy indeed.

I am starting to wish I had abstained from the champagne at lunch. A sip would have sufficed, but Brenda is infectious in her joy and such moments should always be marked somehow. The booze sits in my stomach. I will have to pull it in for the pictures.

Premieres are always horrendous. The prep involved is just too much. I have exfoliated, waxed and applied make-up to most parts of my body. A make-up artist and a hairdresser came over to our house and made me look camera-ready. Designers sent me clothes months in advance. Due to my workouts and my strict health diet, the clothes actually fit. The standards of beauty infuriate me. Men just put on a suit.

I look down at the nude shoes my stylist gave me. They look like biscuit next to my pale skin. More a brown-pink than anything. I am wearing a silver dress with tassels which makes me look like a flapper. My hair is huge and wavy thanks to a ton of styling and extensions. I also have eyelash extensions and an inch of make-up on. I look thin, too thin. I am past that point where it looks good but on camera, I will look much bigger. That is the hardest thing about being an actor. The camera really does add ten pounds. I remember years ago doing a small part in a film and seeing that the actress, who constantly got called fat in the press and looked like she was a size fourteen, was actually tiny in person. It has got a bit better over the years but the pressure to stay in shape never goes away.

When we arrive, my stomach is in knots. The driver comes around and opens the door. William gets out first like he always does. He turns back and puts his hand out. He looks stunning in his Armani suit. An investment that has paid off. I fall in love with him again, he is such a gentleman. I take his hand and make sure I keep my knees together. The bulbs flash as soon as I am out. I smooth my dress down and start to walk. I am arm-in-arm with William until it is my turn to go to the X on the red carpet that each actor has to stand on for the perfect shot. I move slightly to the side and put my arm on my right hip. I give the slightest of smiles. It is a pose that works for me. A number of the paparazzi shout my name and I move from side to side, trying to give them all a good shot. I am popular with the press because I always play the red-carpet game to perfection. It has taken years of practice but I have it down perfectly. It does not take that long and I move on.

William gives me a kiss and hands my bag back to me. I can tell he is proud. We walk down the carpet hand-in-hand.

The film is not great. Still, my friend directed it and before we leave, I will lie to him and say it was brilliant. Bullshit runs our business. I work the room with William beside me, a constant rock. I manage to work the entire room in an hour and then we head back out. As I leave there is a different bunch of paparazzi and they get on the floor to get an upskirt picture of me. They do it to all the actresses. I bite my lip because otherwise I might cry. I hate this. They start calling me names, the c word, a bitch. I see William's jaw tense. He knows not to react because that is what they want. If he punched them, it would be like they won the lottery. If I react, the same.

It puts a downer on the end of an amazing evening. We try and hold it together as we rush to the car. It is late now, so we head back to the children. Not that they will be up, but Brenda probably wants to go home now. She stays over sometimes but I know she prefers her own bed.

William's dad, Ted, is also an old-fashioned guy and, by that, I mean that he is just like a big baby that Brenda has to take care of. Men of that generation just had wives as unpaid domestic slaves. Feminism came and yet the situation didn't change. If I have to hear Ted go on about our 'modern set up' one more time, I might scream.

I put my head on William's shoulder as we drive back. I will not let the horrible paparazzi at the end ruin our evening. I push them away from my mind and smile.

# Chapter 11

## Then

Claudia is on the television and Scarlet is in LA. Here I am sitting in my mouldy house share, surrounded by arseholes, and doing auditions for film students who can barely point a fucking camera. Despondency has been the word of the weekend. Everyone has left me behind. I feel like I will never make it. Not even as a working actress. Or a part-time one. I start to think about other things I can do with my life which will make me just as happy. There is nothing. Acting is the be all and end all. The thought of going to do some office job is too painful.

I have been working in a clothes shop on Oxford Street, folding clothes in the back rooms. The guy I am working with is so particular and wants me to fold them a specific way. Problem is, I cannot see how different my way is to his. They look the same to me, not so much to this guy. I am trying my best but I can tell I am just frustrating him.

On the opening night of the store, we worked all day and night and then we were escorted out of the back by security as the celebrities arrived, least we disturb those gods. I saw the paparazzi outside as I walked to get my bus the long way round. Shouting men with absurdly long lenses. I recognised one actress; a tall, skinny ex-model who was in everything at the moment. I am not a skinny, super-tall model. I cannot believe how thin her legs are. It seems impossible that they can hold her up. She looks like Bambi. I wonder how it feels to look so perfect. I exercise all the time and I still look dumpy.

Towards the end of my shift, I actually started praying for an acting job to come and save me. I have had two auditions in the past month. One for a commercial that pays seven thousand pounds for one day's work and another one for a film that pays barely anything. Either would do.

When I arrive, there is a letter from the landlord on the table. He is putting the rent up. I hold my breath for a second but then I think, no. We pay this guy in cash and the house is dangerous. I doubt he is paying tax on his earnings. Immediately, I email him telling him that he can put up the rent if I can pay it into his bank account, and if he fixes the various problems in the house. It does not take him long to email me back saying he will not be raising the rent after all. Funny that.

I make a cup of tea and then sit down in the wicker chair that is in the kitchen. It is covered in cushions and so comfortable it feels like being hugged. I close my eyes and take a deep breath in. Ah, I needed this. Some calm to my day. I stay there and look out of the window. The sun feels warm on my face.

My phone vibrates in my pocket. I look at the screen. It is my agent. I immediately snap to it and answer.

'Natasha! Great news! You got the film. You start filming tomorrow.'

'Tomorrow! That's amazing. Thank you so much.'

I am elated. To think I was going to dump Richard as an agent now that I have Louise. I feel bad now. The industry is cyclical. It's not his fault.

I will have to hand in my notice. Or take some holiday, or call in sick or something. I do not even care. Fuck them and their crappy job! I am an actor again.

They drive me to set and back. Yes, that feels about right. I feel like a queen. When we arrive on set, I feel as if I am exactly where I belong. I go to make-up and learn the latest gossip about the industry. The make-up artists know everything and are never discreet. There is an actress two seats down from me who is having her breasts painted. Ah, memories of fun times. Not. That will never be me again. I know it will affect my career, and yet I do not care.

I head straight to costume after my make-up is done. I am on set in barely any time at all. I am playing a counsellor today who is running an AA meeting. It is for an edgy drama one of the main television channels is doing. The pay is not great but it is still a lot more than the seven pound an hour I was making folding clothes all day.

We do not run through the scene; we just go for it.

It feels great to be acting again. I am in my element and the entire scene flows. The scene ends with my co-star, an overweight man in his sixties that I recognise from a few things, hugging me. As he does so, he presses himself against my body in an uncomfortable way and his hands slide all the way down almost to my bottom. I freeze. Did anyone else see that? The director yells cut. I look around. No reaction from anyone else. I decide to let it go. The director wants to go again. Great. I get the feeling this is going to be a long day.

It is a long day indeed. It feels like hours until lunch is called. I line up with everyone else. A chalkboard outside the food van lets us know that today's offerings are salsa chicken with couscous or mushroom risotto. I get the risotto. It tastes awful; chewy and dry. I force it down with a cup of tea that I put sugar in for once. I need something sweet to get through this day.

To my horror, handsy sits down beside me and gives me a wink. I am about to get up but I do not want to appear rude, to other people, not him. I could not care less what he thinks. Another actor sits opposite us and they start talking. Handsy has decided that his teenage daughter's friends are all in love with him.

'It's so uncomfortable for me. I just want a woman in my age range, between twenty-five and fifty.'

He turns and looks at me as he says this. I feel hot bile in my throat. This man disgusts me. Who the hell does he think he is? I look around but, again, there is no one there to witness this and I do not want to make a fuss. Images of folding the same pair of jeans over and over again come to my mind. Men like this are just a necessary evil. I do not have any power. Not yet anyway. I shift away from this man as subtly as I can. This film is a stepping stone to something better. I will focus on that instead of worrying how I get from here to somewhere else.

The next scene is much the same. I could punch him in the face, I really could. I can't believe I have to spend the entire day filming with this fat, sixty-something leech who will not stop hitting on me. He keeps asking me inappropriate questions and he really seemed to think he had a chance. This is more than I can take, it is more than anyone should have to take. I will not let him cop another feel. Each time I grab his hands at the crucial moment and push them back up. I have to hug him again in this scene. A proper hug. Pressing my body against him makes me feel nauseous. Even more so when I have to put my hands behind my back to stop the sexual assault, therefore pressing my body against him even more.

The icing on the cake is his body odour, which leaves a lot to be desired. I feel ill. Today was supposed to be a good day, a turning point. I feel overwhelmingly sad. Keeping my dignity has been like wrestling an octopus. There has to be more than this. I want to do great work. Not be a piece of meat that sexist dinosaurs think it is okay to abuse. After all the attempted groping and sexual harassment, I am in a bad mood. I force myself to smile and not let that creep get to me. I do not want to make other people feel uncomfortable, or think I am difficult to work with.

During a break, I stand next to another actor, Greg, who seems like a nice guy, although the barometer is low at the moment. A text comes through on my phone and Greg asks if it is my boyfriend. I loudly ask him how he knew I had a boyfriend, hoping the pervert will hear.

'Of course, you have a boyfriend,' Greg says, giving me an appreciative look. 'I mean, look at you.' He is practically licking his lips. This upsets the only other actress in the scene, Cat, who is walking past and loudly declares how annoyed she is that no one has assumed she has a boyfriend.

'I could have a boyfriend,' Cat keeps muttering.

This day could not get any worse, but at least when Greg hit on me, he stayed on the right side of creepy. As for Cat, her problems have nothing to do with me. I just ignore her and the evil eye she keeps giving me.

Today has not been a good day. I had such high hopes and they all came crashing down.

I stay professional, shaking everyone's hand except the perverts and making sure I leave smiling. Reputation is important in this business and I was pretty sure that I am one of the few people on today's set that anyone will want to work with again.

My driver drops me back at my grotty house share. Usually this feels like an anti-climax and I just potter around not knowing what to do with myself. This time everything feels different. I walk up the stairs to my bedroom and I crawl into my warm bed. I switch on the television and I stay there for the rest of the evening, only moving to order a takeaway.

# Chapter 12

# Now

'The problem is that people are too intimated to work with you. You just won an Oscar, for God's sake,' Scarlet tells me, an airy tone to her voice.

I blink at this comment.

'Then you worked on A Long Road with the Old Master, and who would want to direct you after that?' Scarlet adds another helpful comment.

I let out a sigh. It never stops. The constant fight to get to the top and then stay there. The entire world is one big climb.

'But you should be happy because you have prestige. You cannot buy that. You're so lucky. I wish I had been given what you have been given. Even a tenth of it.'

"Lucky", "given" – these words, coming from Scarlet's mouth are like pellets of rage, hitting me at my softest centre. I can usually take her victim attitude and complete lack of self-awareness quite well but today I do not have it in me. I just let her run off her mouth and zone out. I look into our garden. It is huge and has a big trampoline in it. It also has a swing and a sand pit. There is an apple tree at the bottom. We have a gardener who keeps it in top shape. We even grow tomatoes, potatoes and courgettes. It is a perfect slice of England.

There are a few other words I catch from Scarlet, who thinks she is an expert because she lives in LA now; "millionaire" and "money". If only she knew, how little I earn after I pay off my manager, my agent and the tax man. Running my life is expensive. I am brought back to my phone call with Scarlet when her tone changes.

'Do you remember that famous producer? The one we all saw in Cannes at one point?'

'Robert Hervey?'

'Yeah, the one that shouted at Claudia because she wore a trouser suit to one of his premieres when she had that tiny role in one of his films.'

'I remember him. Everyone knows him, Scarlet. He owns most of Hollywood, or has worked with them anyway. What about him?'

'Well, I met him.'

'I know.'

'Again.'

'Okay.'

There is silence on the other end of the line. I get a fluttering feeling in my chest.

'What is it, Scarlet? He didn't hurt you, did he? Are you okay?'

'Oh, I'm fine. He was just a bit weird and inappropriate, that is all. It just is what it is. All these men always try and have a go. They think they may as well. The film industry is a meat market.' Scarlet laughs a hollow

106

laugh. I want to hug her. I want to hop on a plane right now and envelope her in love.

'What do you want me to do? What do you need? I'm so worried about you.'

'Do not be silly. He didn't rape me or anything. It was not that bad. Forget I said anything.'

'Have you spoken to Claudia?'

'No and I do not want to. I have decided I just want to forget about it.'

'Okay, but if you change your mind, let me know, okay?'

'I will. Promise.'

Scarlet hangs up and I stand there for the longest time, just looking at my phone.

I do not tell Claudia what Scarlet told me. I would never betray her confidence, but it makes me worry about both of my friends. There is a rot in our industry. It spreads from the top all the way down. I think about all the men who put their hands on me, all the sex scenes that I have done where the man enjoyed it a little too much, and the one where a woman did.

I once went for a job interview as a hostess at a club in Mayfair only to find out it was a strip club. I remember auditioning to be a fittings model and having a woman act inappropriately towards me, asking to take my picture when I was wearing a bra. I always thought I could never say no. We all do, because we can't. We are not the ones with the power. Our names end up on blacklists and our careers end. Or we decide we are sick of the abuse and give up. But nothing changes.

I think of my daughter. I would never want her to be an actor. Not in a million years. I would not want my son to be one either, but it is a different thing. I sit and I think of fight or flight. Do I stay and change the industry, or should I leave in protest? But to leave without exposing the reasons for leaving would not be a win at all. It would be giving into the system, it would mean that all the women coming up behind me would end up just as damaged, with the same painful memories running over and over in their heads.

'Are you okay?'

William stands in the door. Handsome and strong. One of the good ones.

*'Uh huh!'*

'You are deep in thought.'

'I'm just thinking about the industry.'

'You don't look as if you are happy with it.'

'I'm not, I don't think women get treated particularly well.'

'Sadly, women rarely do.'

This is why I love him, a human rights lawyer who calls out injustice when he sees it.

'Scarlet had a bad experience with a producer. A famous one.'

'Robert Hervey?'

I look at him, shocked.

'How could you possibly know?'

'I have heard rumours.'

'I haven't and I work in the industry.'

'Well, you've never worked with him. Or auditioned for him.'

'No, but I met him once.'

'You did?'

It is William's turn to be shocked.

'You never mentioned that.'

'It was in Cannes with Scarlet and Claudia. He had a massive go at Claudia because she wore a suit to a premiere of one of his films. She had a small part in it.'

'I forgot she worked with him.'

I try to think what his expression is now but I cannot place it.

'You know he rapes women.'

I do a sharp inhale. I cannot believe what I am hearing.

'Then he makes them sign NDAs. He also goes out of his way to get his picture taken with them after. He is a real manipulative monster.'

I feel dizzy. I thought things were bad but not as bad as this. How can we fix an industry that is this broken?

'He never hurt you, did he?'

'No. I was never alone with him.'

'Good.'

'How do you know this?'

'I can't really say. I did hear some gossip about him at some showbiz parties. He offers roles for massages and such.'

I almost puke. The casting couch exists.

'Maybe, all that only happens over the pond. Maybe in the UK we are better people.' I look at William, hopeful.

'I hope so, darling. I am glad we had this chat. I have always worried that you might have had some bad experiences. You can always talk to me.'

I look at William. A little part of me feels ashamed. I would never submit to the casting couch. Could he have ever thought I might? That that stuff happens here too? I feel embarrassed to be an actress, to be in this disgusting industry but then I realise I am pointing my anger in the wrong direction and I have to throw my shame away. I cannot internalise all this shit. That is what the patriarchy wants. If I blame myself and get embarrassed, I will not change anything. I must direct all of this the other way. I need to change things.

I have only worked once this year. On A Long Road. I have read dozens of scripts and they all depressed me. Most of them were nudity heavy and I was sick of all that. Others had me playing the mother of actors not much younger than me. Most had me playing the girlfriend, wife, or mother. None of them really spoke to me or about my experience as a woman.

Yet I knew I had to work soon. If I did not, people would forget all about me and I might not be able to ever make a comeback. A comeback for an industry I have fallen out of love with, but what else could I do? I have worked so hard to be here and I love telling stories.

Eventually I move on from the scripts and I turn to books. How hard could it be to turn one of these into a film? I could be an ethical producer. I am sure it was Gandhi who said, 'Be the change you want to see in the world.' Or something like that anyway. I call Claudia. She picks up on the first ring.

'We always say we're going to work together,' I tell her.

'We do, indeed.'

'Then we never do.'

'Well, no one has hired us for the same job yet.'

'But why do we have to wait?'

'What do you mean?'

'Let's make our own film.'

'Oh, dude, that is a lot of work,' Claudia responds, clearly not feeling it.

'Who cares! We can do it. Are you not sick of either waiting around for the phone to ring or being offered complete shit?'

There is a pause on the other end and I can tell she is thinking.

'Okay, let's do this.'

I let out a triumphant scream. Claudia has said, yes. I knew she would. She is the most 'fuck it' person I have ever met in my life. She jumps into life wholeheartedly.

'Should we ask Scarlet to join us too?'

'Tash, we're going to need all the help we can get, honestly.'

I dial in Scarlet.

'Hello?'

She sounds blurry, sleepy. It must be night-time in LA.

'It's us!'

'Who?'

'It's us, Scar. Tash has had this great idea that we should make our own films. Screw the rest of them. It's time we took control.'

'What do you say, Scarlet? We can finally change the industry. From the inside out. We need to spin gold out of this hard life, just like Beyoncé's grandmother,' I joke. Claudia laughs.

We hear a muffled yes in-between Scarlet's sobs. Claudia thinks they are tears of joy, but I know the truth.

# Chapter 13

## Then

'All work and no play and that.'

That had been the line Claudia uttered that brought me to this horror; speed dating. We are in a dungeon in central London which is playing cheesy music and selling overpriced cocktails. It is a meat market with a slice of cheese.

'You are so miserable all the time. You need to do something other than worry about your career,' Claudia tells me. I know she is right but I find her comment irritating.

'I'm not miserable all the time. Take that back.'

'Okay, but sometimes you are miserable for an entire day.'

'Because something bad has happened!'

'You need to bounce back more, Tash. You need a good bonking, darling. There is not much a good fuck cannot solve.'

I choke a little on my drink.

The music stops and we are told to take our seats. I walk to mine filled with dread. I have been in a bubble since I left drama school. Either I am working some crap survival job, auditioning, or acting. The only people who take me away from this are Claudia or Scarlet, who does it virtually.

I smooth down my blue dress. The material seems to electrify as I do. I still do not have enough money for good clothes. I should have borrowed something from Claudia. I feel exposed. I do not know how to talk to men. I am hopeless in social situations. I think back to when I lost my virginity. I was nineteen years old and he was the son of my mother's best friend. I thought I was in love with him. After we slept together, he just disappeared. That taught me what I needed to know, but the lesson didn't stay with me – other men would go on to break my heart. I have pretty much given up on love. It feels like something that is too far away. Yet I feel so alone I cry sometimes. Especially on weekends. Sundays are the worst. Other people with their families kill me. Even groups of friends can hurt. I Skype my family sometimes, but it is not the same.

The bell rings. The first guy looks like a younger, thinner Bill Gates. Claudia will be all over him. She has a weird obsession with geeks. She is obsessed with anything Silicon Valley. Her last boyfriend looked like Clark Kent. I smile at him and try to get some words out.

'Hi,' the guy says. 'I am Ben.'

'Hi Ben, I am Natasha.'

'Cool name.'

'Thanks.'

'Ben is a cool name too.'

'Thanks.'

'What do you do for a living?'

'I'm an actress.'

His eyebrows shoot up.

'Wow! That is cool.' He winces because he said "cool" again.

'What do you do?'

'I work in politics.'

It is my turn to be surprised.

'That is' – I pause, give a little laugh – 'cool.'

He laughs too. Then the bell rings and he moves on. They are all like this, only with less spark. I am about to give up when a tall and lanky man sits down opposite me. He has striking green eyes and gorgeous full lips. He has a killer smile and an aura of confidence. He is hot, too hot. I do not trust men who are too good-looking. We do the dance.

'I'm William.'

'Natasha.'

'I'm a lawyer.'

'I'm an actress.'

'Cool job.'

'Cool job.'

But this one is different. It is not a spark, it is a flame.

We spend the rest of the five minutes smiling at each other. I can see his disappointment when the bell rings and it is time to go. The rest of the musical chairs seems to happen on mute.

When it is over Claudia bounds up to me.

'There were quite a few hotties. So glad that we did this.'

I am only half-listening, I am trying to locate where William went.

'Are you looking for someone?' Claudia smirks. She knows me so well.

'Possibly.'

'Oh my God! Point him out.'

We are both scanning the room now. I cannot see him. Claudia can feel my worry and strokes my arm.

'Don't worry. At the end people tick the box of who they liked, then if you ticked each other contact details are exchanged.'

I knew this. He was the only one I ticked.

'Where do I find out if he ticked me?'

'Over there.'

I follow Claudia and hurriedly look for my name and William's name.

'Oh good. You ticked me.'

I jump. It is him. Right beside me. I lose the ability to speak as he smiles at me.

'Would you like to go and get a drink?'

I am about to say I am with a friend and I can't, but then I realise that Claudia is gone.

'I would love that.'

'Good.'

We walk out into the brazing winter air. I shiver. William takes his jacket off and puts it over my shoulders. I think I might marry him right here and now.

'Thank you.'

'No worries.'

We walk along the street.

'You know, this bar here is great. They have food too.'

'It looks great.'

We go in and order drinks. A mojito for me and a beer for him. We sit in silence for a moment, looking at each other.

'I'm glad you ticked me. My friend Claudia dragged me there. I didn't want to go.'

'I'm happy that you did too.'

He is so calm, so steady. Suddenly I find my social ineptness slip away. We talk about everything; our families, our hopes for the future, what we hate. We talk until it is the last order and then we order a taxi. One taxi. We go back to his place. I don't want to subject him to mine.

After another drink, he takes my hand and leads me to the bedroom. His lips are so soft. He kisses me deeply while taking off my dress. He kisses my neck and my breasts, taking time to pay a lot of attention to my nipples. He kisses all the way down until he gets to my pussy. Then he lifts my leg up and on his shoulder. I put my hand on his other shoulder for support. He fucks me with his tongue slowly while his fingers gently stroke my clit. I let out moan after moan. I never thought sex could feel like this. I have three orgasms in a row.

When he finishes, I rush to my knees, eager to return the favour but he lifts me and puts me on his bed. Then he fucks me. His penis is perfect. I have never felt such pleasure in my life. He has an orgasm and collapses on top of me. The weight of his naked body on mine is heaven. I want to stay here forever. This is the happiest I have ever been in my life.

I end up staying the entire weekend. We fuck about six times a day. Each moment is spent discovering each other in every way. We cannot get enough of each other. This is what falling in love feels like. A mad rush over a waterfall. Total immersion.

# Chapter 14

## Then

The next wave of auditions are all commercial auditions. I do not complain because I need the money. I keep trying to sell out. The problem is that no one is buying. Commercial auditions are usually easy; in, grin, out. They take a few minutes and consisted of saying your name, age and agent to camera. They are not scary like theatre or film auditions. There is money at stake but not career progression. Art and commerce rarely meet. I do a few of them a week while I walk around in a haze. I am so happy. I feel like nothing can bring me down. I do not remember having anything else to live for other than acting. Now all I think about is him.

Something has lifted in me. The desperation has gone. I still want every part but the world does not come crashing down when I don't. Now I realise that I have not been living life. All I thought about was making it as an actress. It was the be all and end all.

I have not been allowing myself to be present. I was just constantly focusing on the next thing, when you want the part so badly, they can smell the desperation. It leaks from your pores. I am not desperate any more. My entire world has opened up.

I was right to think the stink of desperation had left me. They want to see me again. When I get a callback, I go over the original audition relentlessly. I wear the same thing and make sure I give a performance with a similar tone. If I book this, it will pay my rent for the entire year. I try to not think about how nice it would be to not have to worry about money for that length of time. Commercials rarely pay well these days. Hell, everything rarely pays well these days. The acting industry seems immune to inflation. Unless you are right at the top. Still, only a complete moron would go into acting for the money.

I head to The Green Room in Soho. It is not my first time here. This place is well known amongst actors. It is where the people who are actually worth asking to audition go. The people who book an occasional job and have good agents. Agents who know casting directors and producers. That small circle of people who hire each other over and over again. Then their children. A never-ending circle of nepotism and favourites that has everyone else working ten times as hard just to get a toe in the door. Booking the job is the goal but just being here seems to be an achievement.

I look around but I did not recognise any of the other actors in the room. I love it here, I can feel the buzz, the excitement at what might be possible.

My name is called and I head in. I say hello and shake hands with everyone in the room. We have a quick chat and then I go into the short scene. Just picking up some stuff, pretending I am doing some last-minute shopping.

'That was perfect. Well done!' the casting director, Simone, says.

She is a pretty redhead with a warm smile. I feel amazing inside. Like a proper actor. I am good at this. Maybe I will get this job after all. I leave on a cloud and head home. I send constant messages to William as I do. He always replies immediately. This is love. I know this is love.

It does not take much to clean and tidy up the room I live in. There are people with bigger cupboards. By some miracle, the washing machine is free so I bung in all my clothes at once. I do not separate them by colour or by the label instructions. I did this in front of William and he was appalled, but nothing bad has ever happened to my clothes. I keep my hands busy, all the while hoping the phone will ring and it will either be my agent or the gorgeous man. I tidy, hoover and dust. It takes just over an hour to clean the room thoroughly. I guess living in a tiny room has its benefits.

I sit down, sweating and the phone rings. I rush for it and answer without even looking at the number.

'Hello?'

I film my part the next day. It is like something out of a dream. I am picked up at home and driven to the Cotswolds. I have my own AD and my own make-up artist. Everything is done at a leisurely pace. The costume department consists of two bubbly blonde women who look almost identical. It confuses me that they are not related. I really gel with them. They have a Claudia vibe but they are older and not as posh.

I am wearing a pretty dress, a coat and strappy heels. Between every scene, an assistant appears with a pair of

Ugg boots so my feet do not get sore. When not filming, I sit around and drink tea and read books all day. When it is time to film my scene it is late, but I don't care. This is heaven.

They film the first part and then I am asked by an assistant to follow her. I do what I am told and make my way into a limousine. Inside there are the executives from the advertising company that has commissioned the commercial. They reek of money and glamour.

'Hi, I am Kate and I am from Make and Partners. We want to thank you for all your hard work. It was a no-brainer you got the part, we loved your audition.' The rest of the people in the limo nod at me, huge smiles plastered across their faces.

I beam. Kate then gets an envelope out of her bag.

'This is your fee minus the buyout. It is for the day. It is two thousand and seven hundred pounds.' Kate looks at me as she says this. I can hardly take it in. I feel she is waiting for me to say something but my brain is mush. I have never seen this amount of money before in my life. Ever.

'I will count it for you.' Kate counts the money into my hand and asks if she has counted correctly. I am not sure. The moment feels surreal and the money is just so much that I can barely comprehend it. Kate looks at me, expectant.

'Let me count it again.'

Kate had miscounted, there was too much by three hundred pounds. She then takes the envelope and puts all the money in and hands it to me. I thank them all and step out of the limousine, wondering if that really happened.

When I get back to the holding area for the actors, a double-decker bus in the middle of a field, I put the envelope in my bag. I am worried that someone might steal it so I bury it deep inside the bag. I finish just in time as the AD calls me for my next scene. By this time, it is one in the morning.

I keep myself awake with copious amounts of cola. The caffeine makes me buzzy and wired but it needs to be done. They decide to improvise and put me in a car, ready to drive into a gas station. When I am in the car and have already driven a little while, one of the assistant directors asks if I can drive. A little too late, but luckily, I can.

For a fleeting moment, I worry about hitting someone with the car. It is dark and I am wearing four-inch heels. The pressure is on, but everyone comes out unscathed.

I ace the scene, which merely consists of me driving into the car park of a petrol station and then we move on to the next. As I wait for the crew to set up the next shot it dawns on me that this might be one of the best and craziest nights of my life.

When the commercial airs I am the main actor in it. I get my buyout and I quit my weekend and my evening job. I log into the actors' directory, Spotlight, and update my credits. It is not looking too shabby. Two feature films, a television show and a few commercials.

The newness of financial security is making me feel grateful for everything. I did not realise how much pressure the constant quest to pay my rent and bills had on me. This must be how the other half live. The ones that never have to worry about money. I can spend my weekends with William now. Our blossoming relationship is going well. He works crazy hours but we go out to restaurants in the evening when we can. I am staying at his place more. I love not having to go back to my crappy house share but I start to worry about how the luxury is affecting me. How much it highlights my closeness to poverty and a void of nothingness. What does that James song say again? Something about being able to cope with being poor until you see such riches. I have money in the bank and a few roles under my belt and yet never have I known more that I am a working-class person in a middle-class industry.

# Chapter 15

## Then

'Could you bend over just a little?'

'Sorry?'

'Just pretend to reach for something on that table and bend over. Not too much, make it look suggestive and sexy, but only a little.'

I am glad the casting director and producer are female. Otherwise, this would be even weirder. I lean over, just slightly and try to make it seductive without being too obvious. I hope they do not want someone with a booty. I have lost over two stone and I am a size eight now. I am toned but not round. I pretend to reach for something and block out how ridiculous my profession is.

'That was perfect. We will be in touch.'

I thank them and leave. I am wandering around Harvey Nichols when my agent calls and asks if I can get to set in two hours. She gives me the address. I say yes immediately and make my way to Ealing Studios. Moving to Ealing has paid off numerous times. I film there quite a lot.

I am elated. Maybe, this is why I am merely a working actress; I am not utilising my bottom properly.

Louise sends me the details as I travel. I take a sharp inhale of breath when I see who the director is, Nadia Sharma. I cannot believe my luck. She is the biggest female director there is. I have seen all her films and it has always been my dream to work with her.

I go through all the information and the sides. I am playing a waitress and have barely any lines. It does not matter, there are no small actors, only small parts as the saying in our industry goes.

I arrive at Ealing Studios with sweaty palms. I am so nervous. The sweaty palms are the only part I cannot out-act.

I announce myself to reception and the AD comes to get me. I head to wardrobe immediately and they look me up and down and tell me that I am fine how I am.

'The jeans are tight enough?' One of the costume women asks the other. The other nods.

'Let's just give her an apron. The vest is tight too and the black is a good colour.'

You get used to being a breathing prop when you are an actor. People just talk about you as if you are not there.

When that is all done, I head to make-up. I am only in there thirty minutes, which seems a bit short considering how long they usually take. I am on set in no time. The tray I have to carry is heavy and the lines I have to utter are mundane but none of that matters. The actors in the film are all national treasures. I grew up watching them. The one I am most excited about is Suzanne Thorogood. One of the happiest times in my childhood was when I watched her comedy show on the BBC with my family. We all laughed together and it made me feel as if we were a normal family, however briefly.

A few times I feel as if Suzanne is giving me a filthy look, or looking at me with that look older women sometimes give younger, beautiful women; the one that says, I hate you and I want to destroy you. I brush it away. No way is Suzanne Thorogood that bitter.

I expect this scene will be brief, but I have four lines so that is something. Hopefully one of them will end up on screen. It takes hours to film the scene from various angles. My arms feel like they might drop off. It is the hottest day of the year yet and I am feeling it. Thankfully, Nadia yells, 'Cut!' And, we go to lunch. Just as I am about to leave, I see the nanny bring Nadia's twin babies out. Oh, my ovaries. They are so gorgeous. Nadia is in her forties and she has a successful career and two children. She is my ultimate role model. She has it all.

Lunch is in a gorgeous pub just off Ealing Common. I get in line for the food. The extras, ADs and main actors are all eating together. I love that. I hate hierarchy.

I order some salmon and roast potatoes with veg on the side. It will make me feel virtuous. I say hello to another day player, Lauren, and she says hello back. We moan about how hot it is and then we look for a seat together.

'That table over there looks great,' I say to Lauren and point to a large table right next to the window. It has good sunlight and a brilliant view of the green. Lauren nods.

'How long have you been acting?' I ask Lauren as we walk to the table.

'I'm mostly a dancer. I've been doing this for three years.'

We sit down and take our food off our trays.

'That's cool. I have to work hard at dancing. It does not come naturally to me.'

Lauren laughs.

'That's okay. Not everyone is born good at something. What about you? How long have you been acting?'

I am about to answer when I see Suzanne Thorogood heading our way with an entourage. She is a literal step ahead of them. They are in a pyramid shape. It looks like something out of a movie. This is what it means to be speechless. Lauren follows my gaze and her jaw is on the floor too. They are coming straight for us.

I make a mental note that Danny once worked with her at the National. He said she is amazing and friendly and gave him loads of advice. That would be a good conversation starter.

Now she is heading my way and I can feel my heart leap. Suzanne and her entourage stop right in front of us. There is a silence of thirty seconds that feels longer.

'This is a great table. It's big and right near the window,' Suzanne says, not even starting with a hello.

'Well, you are more than welcome to sit here. There is enough room for you and your friends,' I reply.

Suzanne stares at me. An icy stare that could freeze the Bahamas. This great star wants to sit here, she just doesn't want to sit next to Lauren and me. I feel indignant. This is bullshit. Who does this woman think she is? She may be a famous actor but she certainly has not cured cancer. I cannot stand people who think they are better than other people. I am moving over my dead body.

'It's just such a good table,' Suzanne says again, looking around but avoiding eye contact with either of us. She is leaning in towards me and acting grand. I do not appreciate being mean-girled by a middle-aged woman who should know better. Suzanne gives me one more defiant stare and then swans off with her huge entourage to a smaller, more cluttered table. Bitching as she goes.

Suzanne looks the encapsulation of grumpy and I can hear her complaints about the food, the restaurant we are filming in and everything else that does not meet her obviously high standards. If I ever manage to be as successful as this bitch, I promise to always treat everyone in a decent way. No matter what their job is.

Somerset House. It is one of the most beautiful buildings. I love it. Maybe I will be so rich that one day I will live here. The courtyard is filling up. People have placed their blankets on the ground. Some people even bring champagne.

Tonight is an outdoor screening of the latest film from Sam Whitley. She is a director I am dying to work with. Her work is always edgy and so on point. Proper art. There is far too much nudity in it for my liking, but then I find that female directors tend to have a lot of nudity in their films. I find it weird. I have a nudity clause now anyway so I don't do my own.

I may be young but I am not sure my bones are made for these cobblestones. The blanket is not doing much to help. William does not seem bothered by the lack of comfort. He is inhaling the atmosphere. I need to take him to more experiences like this. I feel guilty. He is so hot yet I have been hiding him at home.

William pours out the champagne and hands me the glass.

'Thank you for bringing me, darling. I'm having a wonderful time.'

'I'll bring you to more events. I have to show you off.'

'Indeed.'

I look around at the other people. I should network but I am not in the mood. Maybe it is enough that I am here, seeing and being seen as they would put it. I see Nadia Sharman. I feel excited that I have worked with her, even if the film is not out yet. Our eyes meet. She stops and reacts, but what was that emotion that crossed her face? I could not tell.

William catches the moment.

'What was that?'

'I'm not sure.' I decide I do not want to be anxious about it. It is probably nothing. 'Let's just enjoy the film.'

So, we do. We enjoy the film and afterwards we listen to the Q&A from the director and Meghan McQueen, one of the most famous actresses in the world. We sit on our blankets and I try to pretend my bones do not hurt by this stage. We drink champagne and mingle and I am filled with happiness. This is where I belong. In London, going to premieres. London is the centre of everything. The creativity in the air fuels me. The only place better than London would be LA and, thanks to self-tapes, I do not need to move there. Not yet anyway. No, I am perfectly happy where I am.

After the film, we mingle for a while and I go to grab more champagne as William follows. William is in his element. It helps that he looks like a movie star himself. He could easily play James Bond. Especially in that tux that I want to rip off him. We network the room a bit more and then we go home and I do just that.

# Chapter 16

## Now

The interview I did ages ago with Imogen turns out to be a hatchet job. No, scrub that, an assassination. It takes me a moment to start breathing again after I finish reading it. I forgot you can never trust anyone. Especially not a journalist. They are some of the most brutal people I have ever met in my life. Everything is copy to them.

I think back to when I won the Oscar. It was the perfect night. William was there with the children. Claudia and Scarlet too. My inner circle, my family at the pinnacle of my career.

Yet everything has stalled since. The scripts are terrible or the money is. I have to only say yes to what I am worth; both financially and based on my talent. I think back to what Scarlet said, that it was only because everyone was intimidated. She said that no one wanted to direct me straight after one of the most respected film directors in the world had.

Did the men have the same problem? The men who get paid at least double what women do. Are people 'too intimidated' to work with them?

I walk up the stairs to the bathroom, passing the children in their playroom on the way. They are happy playing Lego. I knock before I enter.

'Hello, darling. Want to join me?' William asks.

'The piece came out in Vanities magazine.'

'Ah, I can tell from your face this is not a social call.'

'Natasha Jones is that cliché of a thing; an ageing actress whose career has floundered.'

'Ageing? You are in your thirties.'

'Any actress heading towards forty knows that time is running out and she seems unable to utilise her past success into a career that is anything less than mediocre. It is sad to see a star that burnt so bright fizzle out so soon.'

I want to read the entire article to him but my legs go and then the tears come. I keep thinking with every step on the ladder I will become untouchable. That my career will finally become established. Everyone will want to work with me, and I will never have to worry again. But there is always someone there ready to take me down. The fight is constant and the struggle never ends.

William gets out of the bath and gives me a wet hug. I press myself into his naked body and he envelopes me.

'Do you remember when we broke up?' I ask William.

'Which time, darling? I recall you have dumped me more than once.'

I laugh. 'I never really dumped you. I just got stressed and panicked.'

'Well, now you tell me. That will help with the chip on my shoulder.'

'You said I had changed and you hated me.'

'That was during an argument.'

'An argument that lasted for three months.'

'We have been together for twelve years Natasha. Our marriage will have its ups and downs but you do not need to worry. We are solid. We love each other and we have two children.'

I put my head on his shoulder and let the tears come.

'I was thinking of starting a production company with the girls.'

'You should. Then you will have the power of your career in your hands. Also, you just worked on A Long Road. Fuck her. I never liked Imogen. People who are that cloyingly sweet always have another side to them.'

'You're right. You always are. What would I do without you.'

'Have tons of cats probably.'

'Hmm. You are getting too cocky. I could have pulled someone else.'

'Yeah, they wouldn't have been as great as me, though. Anyway, talking about cocky.' He raises an eyebrow at me.

'Okay, but make it quick.'

'Excellent. Quick is when I am at my best.'

I laugh and lock the door.


We launch Flower productions but we do not make it public to start with. We read book after book and then buy options for the ones we love. The first book we option is a story of three women in a small town who become friends. It has murder and intrigue. I talk to everyone I know and trust; producers, directors, cinematographers, writers. I read Variety, the Hollywood Reporter and Entertainment Weekly. Claudia and I go on a short film course. I am determined to make this a success. Fuck Imogen. Fuck everyone who thinks I am ageing and my career is over.

We are in a sexist, ageist industry and I want to change it.

'I think we should produce a vampire movie. Vampires are so in, right now.' Claudia has her heart set on playing a vampire.

'We could but maybe we want to be more original for our first two projects. Then we can go more commercial; vampire movies, romantic comedies, the lot.'

I can see Claudia thinking about it. She does this thing where she wrinkles her nose a little when she is thinking hard.

'So, the sexy, small town drama it is.'

I have a good feeling about it.

I get offered a part in a romantic comedy and I take it immediately. William sulks that I will be acting opposite Martin Daniels, the sexiest and most handsome actor working today. According to the internet anyway.

'Come with me.'

'What?'

'It's the summer holidays. The children have no school for six weeks.'

I can see him thinking about it. He is a partner at his law firm. They have offices in LA. He could swing it, I reckon.

'It might be nice to have a break. Not sure about hanging out in a trailer on a film set while my wife makes out with a hunk, though.'

I laugh at his use of the word 'hunk' Do people still say that?

'Think about it. You could try and move your work to LA for a while. We could surf and go on hikes in the Canyon. It would be fun.'

I can see him swaying.

'Okay, let's do it.'

I feel happy. The worst part of my career is being away from my family so much. If my family come to LA, I have the best of both worlds.

I don't have the courage to tell Claudia face-to-face. My cowardice kills me because I know she deserves better. Yet, it does not stop me. I have a gin and tonic and then I pick up the phone. She is quiet for the longest time.

'I thought we were starting a production company. I thought we were going to work together and change the world. You said no romantic comedies and the next thing you are off thousands of miles away filming one.'

'I meant for our production company. We can do this anywhere. I never said I wouldn't work. I need to work, Claudia.'

She laughs at this. It is a vicious laugh which surprises me. I have never heard her laugh like that before. We never argue like this. Claudia is always happy for me.

'Come on, Claudia. We're not like this.'

I can hear a change in her voice. Her tone becomes colder. 'What do you mean? Like what?'

'Mean to each other. We do not argue like this. We are always happy for each other.'

I hear a sharp inhale of breath. I can feel her hate on me like a laser.

'No, Natasha, we are always happy for you, with the house and the kids and the career. You are the one with everything and, do not pretend, you need the money.'

I recoil.

'Of course, I need the money. Do you think my lifestyle is free? It costs a fortune. I have staff, Claudia.'

'Oh, I have staff. I mean, listen to yourself!'

'I cannot believe this is coming from you, you were born rich. You were given a flat in London. At least I worked for what I have.'

It is Claudia's turn to recoil. I can actually hear her hurt down the line.

'Fuck you, Natasha. You know nothing about me and my life.'

Then she hangs up and I am left wondering what the hell that was about.


Scarlet is happy at least. It has been a year since I last saw her. She collects us at the airport in an eight-seater car. 'My soccer-mum car,' she calls it. It is a rental but she thinks she might buy one.

I sit in the passenger seat and watch her as she drives. She is tiny. Her wrists look like they might break. Her face looks like it is truly glowing from the inside and there seems to be a suspicious lack of wrinkles. I know she gets work done because she told me but she was vague about exactly what.

'It wasn't a choice, the studio insisted' – she had said, mentioning – 'a few fillers and such.'

I was shocked. Apparently, they do that, insist you get a nip and a tuck, or lose a certain amount of weight. It is all in the contract. Jeez, what an industry. Then actors do interviews and say they have good genes, a fast metabolism and never exercise. It is all smoke and mirrors and the smoke is particularly toxic.

Somewhere there is a girl in Birmingham or Oklahoma who is starving herself because she has no idea that the existing standard of beauty is an impossibility. The thought fills me with shame. I am just as much a part of this.

'Should we stop for an In and Out burger?'

'Yes,' William and the children all yell out at once. I laugh. They love In and Out burgers.

'What a great idea, Scar! It's our ritual, isn't it?'

'It is, indeed.'

Instead of the drive thru, we go into the restaurant. A few people seem to recognise me, but this is LA so no one says anything or disturbs me.

Scarlet goes up and asks for our usual order. Burgers, fries and milkshakes for all. I am sure a few people recognise her too.

I go to help her bring the food over. It is a feast.

'So how is life, Scarlet?' William asks with a guarded tone. I appreciate him making an effort. He has never liked Scarlet. Thankfully, she is not aware enough to notice.

Scarlet finishes her mouthful and then answers William.

'Great, getting parts here and there. There may be a man on the scene.'

'What? I haven't heard about this. Tell me everything right now.'

'It's Alex.'

It takes a moment for my brain to catch up. Then I realise she is talking about Alex. That Alex. My friend Alex.

'Aussie Alex!' I say.

'Hot Alex.'

'Kind Alex.'

'Okay, okay, we get that Alex is amazing.' William is still a little sulky after seeing interviews I did with Alex where we were clearly flirting. I feel bad about it. We had a vicious argument and then we were both working so much. That did not make it okay, of course. It is hard to keep your office flirts secret from your husband when the office is a camera that beams it to the entire world.

'I'm pleased for you. You make a great couple,' I tell Scarlet. I try to ignore that little bit of jealousy that I am feeling and I make sure my congratulations look genuine. My husband is watching me.

'He's so excited that we have started a production company together. He says he's up for any roles. He thinks we are going to do great things.'

I smile. Of course, Alex supports us. He is one of the good men in the film industry. They do exist. Thank God.

'I'm excited about that book that we bought but we need to talk about roles,' Scarlet says, her eyes shooting a warning into me.

Fuck, I never thought about this. The politics of everything. Or how much ego my friends have. Being surrounded by women is starting to feel suffocating. Maybe I should hand in my feminism card and be done with it. I have a vision of a matriarchy and, frankly, it terrifies me. I push this thought away. I cannot internalise it. I can only go forwards. To be that change instead of the problem.

# Chapter 17

## Then

There is a sea of actresses and there is only one role. The exhaustion of the competition wears at me. Who knew there were so many blond actresses, I think ruefully. We are more common than mud.

'Natasha, so glad to see you again.'

I stand up. It's Derek. He came to our end-of-year show and has supported my career ever since.

'So glad to see you, Derek. Thank you for bringing me in.'

'Follow me.'

I follow Derek into a room and I am shocked to see that Ben Hart is there. He is the biggest action hero in the world and has been on top of his game for decades. Despite myself and all of my training I am star struck. The words will not come out of my mouth. I make a weird, strangled noise.

Derek looks at me like I am an alien but Ben is not fazed. He gives me a killer-watt smile of perfect white tombstone teeth. It blows me over again. I finally switch my brain back to human and I take his outstretched hand.

'It's lovely to meet you, Mr Hart.'

'Call me Ben.'

'Ben.'

'Okay, let's run through the scene. I'm sorry, we couldn't give you the script in advance, Natasha, these things are top secret.'

'No worries, and I signed the confidentiality agreement in reception.'

'Great! Let's do this.'

Derek hands me the script and gestures to the sofa. We both sit down.

'And action!'

'Lucy, I want you to come with me. It is not safe for you here. I need to protect you.'

'I do not need your protection, Sam.'

'But you need love.'

'You're right, I do need love.'

Then he kisses me, deeply and with passion. I go with it, even though it feels wrong. William and I are doing well. I think we are in a relationship but we have not had 'the talk' yet. I get that I have to kiss people on film sets but here, in an ordinary, banal office it feels like cheating.

'And cut,' says Ben. He makes a *whoah* sound and looks at Derek who looks back at him and gives him a double thumbs up. They look like two frat boys. I have an uneasy feeling in my tummy. Why am I such a prude? I wish I was more carefree, that I could just go with the flow. Everyone else seems so free.

'You know, you and I, I think we have real chemistry.'

'Should we go one more time? Get it on video?' Derek looks at us both and then leaves his gaze on me for a fraction too long. He is seeking permission. I can only give it.

'Sounds great!' I hear myself say.

'Brilliant, let's do this.' Ben Hart is all energy. He could power the national grid for decades with his enthusiasm and gung-ho attitude. I briefly wonder if he is on drugs.

We do the scene again; the kiss is just as deep with a hint of tongue. His hands decide to go on their own journey. I try to sell this as much as possible but I cannot help but think I am pimping myself out. Derek yells cut.

Ben Hart jumps up like he could make it all the way to the moon. We are done now. I stand up. Ben shakes both of my hands vigorously and so does Derek. I start to say goodbye to Ben and thank him for the opportunity but I can tell he has already moved on. He is huddled over the laptop with Derek. I move my head slightly and I can see they are looking at the head shot of the next actress. I leave, saying a quiet 'goodbye' as I do.

I walk out of Spotlight into Leicester Square. It's buzzing with tourists. I can see that they are setting up for a film premiere. This square is famous. A tiny patch of London that has had the feet of all of Hollywood walk on it. Fans are already lining up to see their film gods. They have phones, pictures and notepads. Autograph hunters and film aficionado. Ben Hart must have walked this square hundreds of times.

I start to wonder if I will ever join them, and as I do, I also wonder if I even want to.

I sit on the sofa in the one relaxing and non-mouldy room in my house share; the living room. It has a reasonably comfy sofa which is covered in a throw that is actually clean, and a large TV. This is all in front of a bay window which is great for people watching. I look at William's profile. I stare at his face a lot. Slowly by surely, I fell in love with that face. Or maybe I did to begin with. It is hard to know where the line is between love and lust in the beginning.

'What made you become a lawyer?'

'Family pressure, money.' He gives a little laugh.

'You come from a family of lawyers?'

'Yes. What about you? What made you become an actress?'

'I fell in love with it. I don't know. I guess I loved stories and films. So, I thought I would give it a shot.'

'You sound less enthusiastic.'

'I don't know. I have already sacrificed a lot. When we were younger, we moved around a lot. My dad was in the military, then I became ill when I was just about to start high school. I got glandular fever. I spent years in bed and a lot of the time the only thing I had the energy to do was read books, or watch films or TV. I fell in love with movies and stories. I have never really felt like I have belonged anywhere. I am not anything so I want to be everything.'

William smiles at me. A pensive look on his face. His green eyes are sparkling.

'Thank you for sharing that with me.'

He lies down on the sofa and puts his arms around me, pulling me down. We stay there for a while, relaxed and happy in each other's arms. I feel loved. I feel like I am home.

'I had to kiss Ben Hart in the audition.'

'Hmm,' William says. I can feel his body tensing.

'It was disgusting.'

'Sure.'

'No, really. Just invasive and weird.'

'What do you mean?'

I look at his handsome face and I fall just a little bit more in love.

'It felt like I was cheating on you. I am William's girlfriend.'

William looks shocked and then happy.

'So, if you are my girlfriend does that mean I am your boyfriend?'

'Yes, of course, silly.'

He kisses me. A kiss one hundred times more amazing than one from a movie star, and just like that we had The Talk.


I gasp as I cross the Atlantic. Even the pain in my ears from the altitude cannot dull this feeling. Who do you think you are? I got asked over and over again. I guess now I have my answer, and they have theirs too.

Two thousand actresses auditioned for the role. My role. I am the chosen one. That is what it feels like. My career was mediocre before this – if it could even be called a career.

The role consists mostly of swishing my hair and pouting my lips. My character gets killed off at the end. It is all very Bond girl and it will make people in Hollywood know I exist. Hell, it will let everyone in the world know I exist.

I was going to stay with Scarlet but then the studio said they would put me up at the Four Seasons. Then when we are in Canada and in the other locations the accommodation will be just as lush. I am living the life.

The studio said I had to lose weight so I did. Two hours of exercise a day plus a strict diet every single day. I lose a stone in two weeks. William did not like it. He didn't think it was normal. I miss him. Tremendously. He is the only thing that is missing.

The flight wears me out but I am still buzzed when we land at LAX. A driver is waiting for me and takes me straight to the hotel. I cannot believe it when I arrive in my 'room.' This is no room. It is an apartment. A family of four could come and live in here. This is as far away from small town Scotland as you can get. I jump onto the bed and starfish. I have made it.

I drop my stuff off and then I walk around the Four Seasons. It is like walking around Madam Tussauds. I make sure I do not react. I do not want to come across as a star fucker. I want to be one of them, not a fan.

I sit at the bar in my jeans and an, admittedly, high-end T-shirt (sixty pounds from Jaguar in their sale) and I do not care. If anything, my converse looks too new. Everybody is done and takes a huge amount of effort with their appearance but it has to look effortless. I get the feeling trying too hard is death in LA.

'Can I get a cosmopolitan?'

Okay, my drinks choice is a bit retro and more suited to New York but I do not care. I am full of joy. Part of me wants to pinch myself. Even though, I have always known I was born for greatness, there is always an insecurity at the core of me. A complete panic that I will be dragged down into the depths. It is sometimes followed by a creeping darkness. I can never sit and relax because I am scared of the nothingness that chases after me. The problem with having something is the fear of losing it.

I close my eyes tightly and reset myself. Not today, Satan, not today. I take my drink and head out to the pool. I find a lounger that is in the shade and I lie down on it and I breathe it in. The people, the city, the buzz. It feels like I have made it and I guess, for the moment, I have.

*Now*

The studio puts us up in a suite at the Standard. It is modern and sexy and I love modern and sexy. For all of William's whining about my career, I know he loves the perks. Having a movie star for a wife makes you interesting.

I think about my first ever time in LA as we unpack. I had been elated when I arrived. It was a dream come true for a small-town girl. Scarlet and I had lots of fun. We had gone on hikes and gone to every place worth going, working the scene with all our might. Scarlet had always networked like a demon. She had the same ruthless pursuit of success that I had but hers had no filter and no boundaries. I got the feeling Scarlet would kill her own mother to make it.

Making the film had been a disappointment. Ben Hart had been endlessly flirty with me. I had mentioned it to William and he had flown out when he could. I brought William to set and introduced him to Ben once. That did not go down well. It gave our interactions an edginess and, yet, did not stop the flirting.

Nothing happened, of course. He referred to me endlessly by my character name with a "juicy" in front of it, "Juicy Lucy". It still makes me shiver now.

I remember reading an interview with a huge Hollywood actress that resonated with me, "My main job on set is dealing with the male actor". The main part of my job was dealing with the sexual harassment that came my way and hoping that it would not turn into anything else. All while nodding and smiling and behaving like a good, obedient girl. All these years later, I still have to deal with this shit.

I think about where the power is in this industry and the truth is, it is in producing and directing. Creating the work is where the power is. That is what I want; power. I am done with being the nice woman.

'You look serious.'

I look up at William and give him a smile.

'I'm just plotting on taking over the world.'

'Of course you are, darling. My fierce and beautiful wife. They better watch out.'

I put my nose against his and we nuzzle. I do not know where I would be without this man. I want to show him how much I love him but the children are in the other room. I should have brought the full-time nanny rather than the part-time one I have written into my contract along with the tutors for the children when it is term-time, but William always wants to be "hands on". I love that about him. He is an amazing father. He is always present with the children. You can never underestimate how amazing it is when you have someone in your life who listens to you.

It is late, so after we unpack, we shower and change into out pyjamas. Then we all watch a movie in bed.

We spend a weekend together, surfing and hiking. It is the calm before the fourteen-hour days. I love making movies but I also hate it. All people who work in the industry do. It is tedious and monotonous. The days are long as hell and it can be terrifying. Like when you have a huge emotional scene where you have to cry. Or you are filming sex scenes and spend twelve hours a day in nude underwear surrounded by hundreds of people. It is the weirdest, most surreal thing. It is also a huge privilege of course, just not a glamorous one.

We bake a cake when we get home from all the exertions and Amelia tells me how much she loves having me around.

It stabs at me and I feel that familiar working mother guilt. Maybe one day I will take her to set with me but I think she will be bored. Sitting around in my trailer is hardly riveting. No matter how much I try to carve out a balance, the work/life thing never works. There is always something out of whack. I have to accept that for what it is.

William gets up at five a.m. to have breakfast with me. I am so touched by his sweet gesture.

'I hope you have fun today kissing two handsome men.' He winks at me as he says this. He knows I hate intimacy with strangers. Or anyone who is not a member of my family. I know he gets a little jealous and I cannot blame him. I would too.

We eat our pancakes and drink our coffee. This moment is perfect.

# Chapter 18

## Then

I come back from LA tanned. I am walking on a cloud. I feel as if I am on the cusp of something big. I will stop having to do shit, stressful auditions and worrying if I will ever work again.

It is winter in London and the air has a Baltic bite to it. The contrast makes me want to fly back across the pond. I am not a winter person. I am wearing three layers and a heavy coat and I am still bloody freezing.

I have promised Claudia I will meet up with her after my audition today and, even rarer, Scarlet is in town. She is doing a play at The Garrick. I feel a twinge of professional jealousy. I have never done theatre and I wonder if I will ever work up the courage. I guess I will have to, if anyone is ever going to take me seriously.

I wander around looking for the address the casting director gave me. It takes ages, but finally I find it. I have zero sense of direction. I look at the buzzer. Very faintly I can see the name of the production company so I press the button. I hear a posh voice on the other end. There is always a posh voice on the other end.

'Come on up, we are on the third floor.'

I walk up the stairs slowly. I do not want to sweat before my audition. I get to the top, thighs burning, and the receptionist gives me a strange look. She hands me the form to fill in without barely looking at me and then comes around and takes a Polaroid picture of me before I can even fix my hair. Okay then.

I fill it in and give it back to her. I have no idea how many of these forms I have done in my life now. Hey, at least it means I am working even if I have to constantly write down my age, ethnicity, dress size, bra size, shoe size, height and "anything else" they should know.

I manage to drink some water before I am called in. The casting director is a gorgeous black woman. She looks at me and smiles and I am almost bowled over. Wow! This woman has charisma – she is on the wrong end of the camera.

'Hi, I'm Sharon.'

'Hi, I'm Natasha.'

'You can put your stuff over there.' She gestures to a chair. I take my coat off and then I worry about how many layers I am wearing. I hope they do not add too many inches.

I put my hand out and she shakes it. I still have not recovered from her mega-watt smile.

'Stand on the X and then say your name, age and agent.'

I do as I am told.

'Excellent, let's go through the scene.'

We go through the scene.

'Perfect! I loved it.'

I stand there. We have only done one take, no direction. She looks at me again.

'You can go now. It was lovely to meet you.'

'Oh, wow! That was quick. Thank you.'

I gather up my stuff and say thanks and bye before I leave. I feel like a socially awkward idiot. I am angry at myself as I descend the stairs. I blew it, I know I did. I was awkward and weird.

My mood does not improve as I meet up with the girls.

'Hi, darling. We are just talking about Scarlet's tits,' Claudia says as she gets up and kisses me on each cheek.

I lean over and give them a squeeze. Both girls laugh.

'They seem fine to me.'

'Fine? Fine?'

Scarlet is doing her best to feign indignation.

'*Ha ha.* I meant glorious and dazzling.'

'Well, that's better.'

The waitress comes over to take my order. Claudia and Scarlet already have their food. Claudia has pasta and wine and Scarlet has soup and wine. I get the gist. I order a wine and a salad. When the waitress leaves, Scarlet resumes her tit talk.

'I have a nude scene. It is my first full frontal and I am trying to get into the best shape.'

I shudder, thinking of my sex scene. It was awful.

Scarlet has stopped talking and I can feel her eyes on me. I am mortified to realise that she thinks I am judging her.

'Oh, love, I'm sure it will be fine. I got mine out once. Seriously, people are not fussy about boobs. Everyone loves them. Yours in particular.'

This seems to make her a little bit happier.

'You do want to do it? I mean, you're my friend. I care about you.'

'These things are never a choice, Tash. They are a price that needs to be paid.'

Claudia looks as uncomfortable as I feel.

'There are actresses that have never done nudity,' I tell Scarlet.

'Only a handful and usually they have a famous last name or some power. You have no power in your early career. They are always going to exploit us. You should know that more than anyone. I mean, they always film the sex scenes on the first day for a reason. So, if the actress says no they can recast immediately.'

It is my turn to be offended. I try not to but it is my sore point. I had no power that day. I was just a puppet going through the motions. I had no idea I could say no. That word was more powerful than I was. In many ways, it still is. Can she not see that I am only giving her the advice I wished she had given me on the day I called her? Yet I know she is right.

Claudia can see my sadness and I can feel her foot rub me under the table. God, I wish I was gay for this girl. She is my best friend in the entire world.

'Well, one day we will have the power. Then we'll not have to take any of their shit.'

Scarlet looks at me and blinks. I can tell she does not believe me.

'Anyway, why is it nudity when a woman is topless but it's fine for a man? They can just walk down the street with their shirts off. Why are our breasts sexualised? It's bullshit. Free the nipple!' Claudia says and then raises her glass.

Scarlet and I raise our glass too and say, 'Free the nipple,' in unison. People look but we do not care. This is followed by a contemplative quiet.

'Claudia says, you have a boyfriend.'

'I do. His name is William.'

'Lucky you. You always land on your feet.'

I ignore the jab. The second jab. It is a good job; Scarlet is like my sister. Otherwise, I would give up on her bullshit.

'Tash is in love with him,' Claudia says and smiles at me.

I am. I have not mentioned it publicly before. It kind of sneaked up on me and I have been too scared to say it out loud, in case I jinx it.

'Where have you come from?' Scarlet asks. She has her scowl on. I know she wants me to fail.

'An audition. It went badly. No way did I get it.'

'Aw, darling, you always think that! I am sure it went well.' Claudia put her hand on my hand and gives it a rub. I do not know why I have to constantly make myself less than them and downplay my successes so Scarlet will be less of a bitch to me. Eric Clapton sang that no one loves you when you are down and out, but they hate you when you are successful too.

'Why don't we have some prosecco? Or go and get some tea and cake at Claridge's? We are together so rarely we really must make the most of it.' Claudia asks.

I force a smile. I will do anything for Claudia and will follow her around like a puppy, even though, I am not feeling it. A heaviness has taken place within me. I do not think I have the energy to lift it.

'I don't have that kind of money. I'm on a budget. Not all of us work all the time,' Scarlet says to me, not even trying to keep the bitterness out of her voice.

'None of us work all the time, Scar.'

She shoots a look at me for this.

'You work pretty consistently.'

I cannot help it any more. I snap.

'Can you please stop being such an awful, jealous bitch. I have had it. It's hard for everyone, not just you!'

This makes Scarlet flounce off. Her coat catches on the chair as she pulls it and it tips right over. She does not bother to pick it back up. People stare. When she is gone, I let out a long, deep, sigh.

'Well, she is in a mood.'

'No, I think that's just her all the time, Claud. She is never happy for anyone, ever.'

'She is going through a rough time. LA is tough as hell. There is something like a quarter of a million actors there. She is waitressing and doing a lot of other awful jobs. Did you see how thin she is?'

I think about it. Was she thin? I hadn't noticed. She was wearing a long-sleeved, floor-length flowery dress. Her fake tits certainly felt round.

The guilt starts to creep up on me. 'I'm going to call her.'

I can see Claudia's face brighten. She hates it when people fall out.

Scarlet picks up straight away. She is crying. I feel awful.

'Sorry.' I hear through the sobs. *Was I too hard on her?* I think I was.

'Oh, Scar, let's not fall out. I'm sorry, I don't want you to be upset. Come back. We don't get to spend much time together. Let's make a day of it.'

I hear an "okay" strangled through the sobs. She is really upset. Hysterical even. Something must be going on. I feel bad that I was so harsh on her.

'I will come back.'

'Good.'

Claudia gives me a thumbs up. I hang up and we wait for her. It does not take long before she arrives, looking like a country mum in her big, floral dress. I can see what Claudia means. Scarlet is all bones. Even her breasts look smaller – I didn't know that could happen when you have implants. Even Claudia, a toned to perfection size eight with perfectly portioned breasts looks big next to her. I hate to think how big I look next to her. I am a size fourteen at heart who struggles to stay the size eight I am now. I think about looking for body hair to see if she has an eating disorder but there is no skin to be seen. Mascara is streaked all the way down her cheeks. I stand up and go to give her a big hug. I stroke her hair and squeeze her. I can tell she is hungry for it. It feels as if she has been starved of love. I think about my friend, all alone over in LA and I feel sad. I should call her more. She is alone trying to make it in a ruthless industry.

I release her and wipe the mascara from her face. She gives me a smile.

'I'm sorry, I was taking things out on you. I will be a better friend,' Scarlet tells me as she rests her head on my shoulder.

'You already are.'

'Right, ladies, I have paid the bill. Let's go and have a picnic. Green Park is near and it is a glorious park. Sound like fun?'

'Yes, it really does,' Scarlet says and adds Claudia to the hug.

We walk out together hand-in-hand, leaving all of the stares and the judgemental looks from people on their lunch breaks and harassed parents behind.

'Wait here,' Claudia says and goes into Pret. She comes out ten minutes later with enough food to feed ten people. I feel a stab of guilt. Claudia always seems to pay for things and it is not fair. I make a mental note to pay the next day out.

We head to the park on this glorious summer's day. I worry that I am not wearing enough sunscreen. I have to keep my skin pale for the roles I am cast in. Never mind the damage the sun does to your skin.

We find a beautiful spot far away enough from other people. It has some shade from a tree which is at peak foliage. I take in the beauty of nature.

'My mum died.'

Claudia and I both look at Scarlet, our mouths hanging open. We are too stunned to speak. Claudia is the first one to break out of it and go over to her. She hugs her and strokes her hair.

'Oh Scar. I had no idea. You poor thing. I should have asked you why you were back in the UK.'

'I am going up to Liverpool tomorrow. That is when the funeral is. It's all so fucked up. I hadn't seen her in ages because I couldn't afford a plane ticket. Now I have emptied out all my savings just so I could see her off. I am in the worst place ever. No back up savings, no Mum. My brothers are being mean to me because they say Mum was heartbroken that I just went to LA and never came back. They say I have forgotten my roots.'

I completely forgot Scarlet was from Liverpool. She was the first to drop her accent at RADA. She took to RP so thoroughly that she sounds more posh than Claudia now.

'Oh, darling! Ignore them. People say awful things when they are grieving.'

I leave Claudia to comfort Scarlet. I have no idea what it is like to lose a parent. It must be awful. I think about my relationship with my family. How rocky it is. They seem to resent me and make bitchy comments all the time, but I love them. I always will. I know deep down that they love me too. Is there anywhere that is more 'home' than your family, than your mother? I do not think so. Scarlet is homeless now. Untethered.

Actors are gypsies but everyone needs something to root them. I try to remember her father. Whether or not he is in the picture. I do not recall her ever mentioning him. Now does not seem like the time to ask.

She does not cry this time. That surprises me. I guess she is all cried out. I pour a drink for us all while Scarlet rests her head on Claudia's lap. The rest of the picnic goes well, but a heaviness hangs over it.

I pack up and head to the bin. As I do, I can hear Scarlet ask Claudia for money. Claudia hates this. Everyone hates this. I see her bristle and her expression change. Scarlet seems oblivious. For an actor she is not that observant of people and their behaviours. I hear Claudia say a tense "yes". I feel sorry for her. When you have something, someone else always wants it. I am starting to think it is better to just either have nothing or be invisible.

We all walk back to Green Park tube together. None of us can think of anything to say. There has been a sombre tone to our entire day despite the blazing sunshine.

We give each other a kiss on the cheek and go to our separate platforms. For once I am glad to head back to my dingy, mouldy house share. Sometimes you just need to be home. No matter how rough it is around the edges.

# Chapter 19

## Now

The best thing about winter is layering up and not having to faff with sun lotion. I sit in Starbucks in Oxford Street with a skinny latte. I can tell some people have noticed me but I pretend not to notice. You become an expert at blocking and ignoring. You even become expert at doing it while not appearing rude. Mostly anyway.

I see someone take my picture but they are pretending they are taking a selfie. That is one of the ways people do it. The other is to pretend they are on their phone but scrolling or reading. But the phone is up too high. I guess they want to save face.

I self-consciously smooth down my hair. No one ever looks good in this type of photo and it could end up anywhere. I think of the tabloids and those celebrity magazines with their circle of shame. I shudder. The pressure to look good is intense for any woman, but for an actress in the spotlight it is magnified a million times. It is not okay to even look normal or real. We are just human beings who are not allowed to be so.

I turn to the window, away from the lenses. I wish I was wearing sunglasses. Who cares that it is winter and raining outside. Posh Spice definitely has the right idea.

Amelia kept having nightmares last night. I am so tired that my eyes hurt and I feel as if I have disgusting bags under my eyes.

I take my phone out to check the time. I can go now. I grab my latte and make my getaway. I had chosen this spot with great care. Quick getaways are my speciality. I leave before anyone even notices. I make my way to the office of Golden Eagle productions. I have been shopping around our ideas and trying to find someone to collaborate with. I have spent so many years on set it would be impossible to count. I have watched and learnt. I know about story and lighting. Best of all, I do not think I know it all. There is always more to learn. Now I have to convince everyone else.

I am glad I wore my Sam Edelman Chelsea boots today. They go great with my skinny black jeans and chunky cable knit sweater which is cinched in with a belt. I am wearing a Burberry trench over the top. It is keeping me somewhat dry. Luckily, I remembered to pack an umbrella which is in my burgundy Mulberry tote.

I have researched Golden Eagle productions and everyone who works in it within an inch of its life. They are not American, surprisingly; London-based and pretty much all English. Most, if not all, went the Oxbridge path. So far, so every day. But they have made some kick-ass TV shows in the past few years with female leads. I need a piece of that action.

I go deep into SOHO. It is such a funny place, with all these production companies with sex shops and strip clubs dotted around. I pass quite a few sex shops and some places I am sure are brothels. One is certainly a strip club. Eventually, thanks to the map on my iPhone, I reach a modern-looking office block. The plaque on the front says "Golden Eagle" productions and it has a golden eagle with its wings spread out on top of the logo. It is all gold. I press the buzzer.

'Hello, Golden Eagle. How can I help you?'

I do not say anything, I just move so I am in the receptionist's eye line and she can see who I am. She practically jumps and then buzzes me in.

'So sorry to keep you waiting, Mrs Jones. What can I get you?'

I see an entire fridge full of Smartwater behind her.

'Water would be great, thank you.'

She takes one out of the fridge and hands it to me in a sweet, giddy way. She is different from other receptionists. She is gorgeous, of course, but also curvy and fashion-forward. Those designer clothes cannot be bought on a receptionist's salary. She has dark brown glossy hair and super cute cheeks. She is clearly wearing false eyelashes which make her look even younger. I reckon she must be twenty-one, if that.

'I am such a fan of your work. I have seen every single one of your films.'

I try not to flinch. There is not an actor in the entire world who wants someone to see every single film they have made. There are always some stinkers in there.

'Thank you, that's so sweet of you. What's your name?'

'Jemima.'

Of course. A posh name for a posh girl.

'It's lovely to meet you, Jemima.'

'You can go up now. They're ready for you. It's the first office on the first floor.'

I get in the lift and head up. There is a flicker of nervousness before I put my game face on. There is everything to play for.

The door to the office is open. I can see Gyles as soon as the lift doors open. He waves at me and I head down. Miles puts his head around the door. Gyles and Miles. It has a ring to it. They both stand up to greet me.

'The famous Natasha Jones. Look at you. Gorgeous as ever.' I have met Gyles before at the BAFTAs.

'Wonderful to meet you, Natasha. I've heard so many great things about you. I love your work.' Miles puts his hand out and I shake it, followed by Gyles.

'The feeling's mutual. I have admired your company for years. The films and TV shows you guys make are the best in the industry.'

Miles and Gyles give each other a smug look. They know they are knocking out hit after hit. Most of their films get nominated for one major award after another.

'So, you told us you have some ideas?' Gyles says with what sounds like amusement. I have a bad feeling that they are not going to take me seriously.

'Well, as you know, the projects out there aren't great. So, I wanted to get some friends together and make our own movies. There is a lack of movies with strong female leads and we want to fill that gap.'

Giles and Miles look at each other again. My stomach starts to knot. They are trying to make me feel like a little girl. I am not a little girl.

'Well, Natasha, the thing is, making movies is quite hard. I mean, getting funding is hard. It is a brutal industry. You making movies with your friends is all well and good, but we run a business.'

I feel hot bile in my mouth. I give myself a moment to respond because I do not want to be rude.

'Also, films with females do not sell,' Myles says.

'You have made films with "females". I accentuate the word "female". They do not seem to notice.

'Well, those are anomalies. Or some franchise or something. I know it can be hard when an actress reaches middle-age.'

'I am thirty-six.'

'Right, so when that happens the roles can dry up. We would be happy to keep you in mind for any roles that come up. We will always offer you an audition.'

An audition. I am an Oscar-winning actress and they are two businessmen in suits. They are both staring at me now. Finally gracing me with an opportunity to say my piece.

'Well, my friends are Scarlet Walsh and Claudia Temperton.' I let that sink in, their eyes light up. 'And I know making movies is hard. I have been doing it for years. We have been reading books and buying options. We already know a lot and are happy to learn more. It's all about hiring the right team. You say that female films don't sell but women are half of the world. We want to go to the

165

cinema and see ourselves. We need to have our stories told. We deserve it.'

They both look at me, mouths open and take it in. In this moment, I cannot feel which way this is going to go. I think I might be sick. These are two of the most powerful men in the industry and they are acting like uneducated sexists.

Eventually, Miles nods. 'Well, that's interesting. That has given us a lot to think about.'

'It really has. Let us think about it and get back to you.' Gyles finishes.

'Of course.' I stand up and give them my best smile. I shake their hands and then I leave. I give Jemima a wave as I walk past her. She is on the phone but beams back at me.

I get an Uber as soon as I leave the building. I want to be home, right now. I need to feel secure, away from this brutal world. It feels like it takes an age for my Uber, even though, it is there within minutes. I manage to keep myself together for the entire drive back but as soon as I get through the door I start to cry. I am so sick of being treated like crap. William comes to me quickly.

'Darling, what is it?'

I put my weight on him as he puts his arms around me. I wipe my eyes.

'Oh, just some posh twats.'

'Hey,' William says. He is also a posh twat. I laugh.

'Sorry,' I manage to get out, but then I laugh again.

'Is this because of your meeting?'

'Yes, they didn't take me seriously. At all. It was awful. They looked down on me and were so condescending. They said movies with females do not sell. They even told me that making movies is hard. As if, I didn't know.'

'Well, they do sound like twats. Come on, off the floor. Let's have a nice lunch together and then think of your next action plan.'

He helps me up and we walk into the kitchen together. 'They called me middle-aged.'

William practically spins around. 'Middle-aged? Jesus, what a horrible industry you're in. You're young and beautiful and perfect.'

He takes my face in his hands and he kisses me. His lips are as gorgeous and soft as they have ever been. I run my hand through his hair and the other one behind his back. We are hot and heavy now. I take my coat off and pull my jumper and T-shirt off. He unbuttons my jeans and then pulls them down. Then he pulls down my knickers.

I am naked now. He looks up at me and I love the look of awe in his face. He finds me beautiful. When I see myself through his eyes, I feel invincible. Like a goddess. He kisses me all over. It feels amazing and I start to moan. He pushes me against the wall and kisses all the way up my stomach and then takes his time with my breasts. Then he kisses my neck while he fingers me. I orgasm quickly. It feels amazing. He lifts me and fucks me up against the wall. It is perfect, glorious abandonment. I dig my nails into his bottom as he ejaculates inside of me. We stay like that for a while. Sweaty and naked in each other's arms as I bury myself in his neck. It is a perfect moment.

'Do you see? You are perfect and beautiful,' he whispers into my ear. 'You are loved.'

*Then*

I look around my room. It is tiny; ten feet by nine. Apart from the sofa bed and the chest of drawers, it is barren. I added a plant last week to try and make it look homely after a friend made a mean comment. The truth is, I do not care what this room looks like. It is not my home. It is a stopgap to somewhere else. The thought of staying here terrifies me. It would mean I never made it.

I log onto Facebook.

*World famous actor and singer, Adam Derrick, has died. Nothing has been made official but the rumours are it was a drug overdose.*

I see this as I scroll through. I am not sad. The rumours that he was a sex pest are boundless. There was even a documentary about it on the BBC. Yet here people are, pouring their heart out for some false God they never even met. The hypocrisy makes me angry. I put together a post.

*Everyone is going on about Adam Derrick but I think we have all heard the rumours about him. Seriously, people, open your eyes!*

I go and make a cup of tea and when I get back to my computer, I have hundreds of likes and comments. I am taken aback as I read them through. Some agree with me but most are downright nasty.

*'I have no idea who you are but thank you for flagging yourself up. I am going to block you now.'*

*'What a heartless bitch.'*

They go on like this. I try to not let it get to me but it feels crappy being abused for pointing out facts. My heart feels like it stops when I see the next post. It is from Graham Turner, one of the biggest casting directors in the entire world. He casts the majority of everything. I added him as a friend and was delighted when he accepted. I add everyone on Facebook. I use it to network and get jobs. Anything to climb up the greasy pole.

'*Your comments are disgusting and insensitive. You should be ashamed of yourself,*' his comment says.

Fuck! What should I do? I have clearly upset one of the most powerful casting directors there is. I panic and send him a private message.

'*Graham, I am so sorry for my comments. I will remove the post immediately. This is an important lesson for me to be more sensitive.*'

I can immediately see dots. My throat tightens.

*'Natasha, there is nothing that will make this okay. I do not accept your apology.'*

Fuck! What now?

I try again. *'I understand. I apologise again and I really mean it. My comment was not okay. I was being stupid.'*

The message pops up quickly. *'Yes, you are.'*

I decide to leave it there. All I can do is hope that he forgets about me. It is not like he would take a note or anything. People do not blacklist anyone in the entertainment industry. Do they?

I get my answer quickly. I get no more auditions from Graham Turner for months. I usually get a lot. A friend of mine works there and I think about asking her if I am on some kind of blacklist. I decide against it because I do not want to put her in an awful position.

After six months, I reply personally to one of Graham's auditions. He emails back within five minutes.

*'Why not, come in for the whore. At our offices, nine a.m.'*

I reread the breakdown. There is no role of 'whore.' I feel a sting in my eye. My career is ruined before it has even begun. All because of some stupid Facebook post.

I have no idea whether I should go or not. My self-respect says no but what if I am just imagining this? What if he is being genuine? Maybe this is *mea culpa*. He wants me to humiliate myself and then I will start getting auditions from his company again.

I cannot read this situation. I have no idea what to do. I put my head in my hands. I am a stupid fuck up. I will spend the rest of my life in this shitty house share on the fringes of London. My career is over before it even began.

The next day, I go to the audition. Graham is wrapped up in a conversation with a striking young man but he clocks me immediately. He gives me a side-eye glare that could kill. I give him a huge, sunny smile and say hello. I will not be bowed. I will not even acknowledge this. I take the audition. Not for the non-existent role of the whore but a quick in-grin-out audition. He is talking to the same guy as I leave and I give him a big wave and say goodbye. He is obviously shocked that I turned up and that I did not wither underneath his power. I leave elated. I am so proud of myself. I may not be cast in anything he works on but I am stronger and better than I have ever been.

# Chapter 20

## Then

'Did you give her the money?'

I can see Claudia's body tense. She does not answer immediately.

We are in her beautiful flat in Notting Hill. It looks like something out of a magazine. Claudia has always had an eye for style. It is a two-bedroom maisonette. She had the modern stainless-steel kitchen ripped out and replaced with wood. The living room has pale grey walls, a dark wooden floor and grey curtains. It also has a gorgeous garden that she plants tomatoes in. Jeez, she is practically domestic. I guess I would be too if I actually had a home rather than a tiny room in a shit hole.

The sofa is dark grey and the cushions are grey. I have made the fifty shades of grey joke more than once. She has the grace to pretend she finds it funny, even though, she must hear it a lot.

'Yes.'

'How much?'

'Five thousand.'

I almost choke on my milkshake.

'Jesus.'

'Indeed.'

I feel sorry for Claudia. Scarlet has clearly used her. I will never lend someone money. Ever.

'I am not sure I want to be her friend any more. She is so one way,' Claudia says. There is a hard edge to her words that I did not realise she was capable of.

'Oh, darling, don't be silly. We have known each other for years. She's fun.'

'Yes, fun but that is it. She is also selfish, self-absorbed and completely unaware. I am sick of it. When was the last time she did anything for anyone else?' Claudia practically spits the words out. Anger punches every syllable.

'I think she's struggling. Her mother just died and she is so thin.' I feel weird that I am the one standing up for Scarlet. It is usually the other way around.

Claudia raises her eyebrows but does not say anything. After a long pause, she looks at me with a serious look I have never seen before.

'Well done for standing up to Graham Turner. He is such a twat and everyone knows it. He is universally hated in this industry. I have no idea how he gets work.'

A snort escapes before I can stop it.

'Really? I thought I was the only one who thought he was a twat.'

'Lucy, who works for him, says he is a massive bully with an ego the size of the entire world.'

I think about this. I thought I was alone and powerless. That I had upset him and this was my fault, when all along he was a bully with a reputation. Actors are the ones with the least power in the industry but maybe if we started talking to each other that would change. Then we would have strength in numbers. There is Equity of course, which is a fantastic union, but I know so many are scared to talk in case they end up on a blacklist.

'There's power in numbers.'

Claudia looks at me, raises an eyebrow as she takes a bite of her Byron burger.

'Think about it. We are the lowest on the totem pole. We are expendable and constantly forced to do things that we do not want to do. Auditions are humiliating. Then every now and then something really bad happens. One of us gets assaulted or something inappropriate happens. Or we get blacklisted or bullied in the workplace. We do not even know that it is a pattern of behaviour. We think it's us, because we have no power, but we lack knowledge.'

'That is what Equity is for. It also pays to be connected. You need to network to get the goss.'

I think about what she just said. She is right, I guess. I dismiss the idea that was growing. It was probably a stupid one anyway.

We finish our burgers, chips and milkshakes and watch the latest Reese Witherspoon film. This is a blissful afternoon with my very best friend. I feel lucky.

'How are things going with William?'

'Great. He is at a football match with some work colleagues.'

'I cannot believe you nabbed a lawyer. Lucky you.'

'What do you mean?' I ask Claudia. I know what she means.

'I mean, the industry you have chosen does not pay very well, does it?'

Shock takes my breath away. I cannot believe I am hearing this from Claudia of all people.

'Well, that's a sexist point of view.'

Claudia spins around.

'Not really, though.'

Claudia and I have never argued before so I tread carefully, despite my anger.

'How not? I pay for everything in my life. William pays for nothing.'

'Oh, come on, Tash. It must have crossed your mind.'

'What?'

'That he has a secure profession with a good salary.'

My reservations evaporate.

'Are you calling me a gold digger?'

'I am not saying you consciously chose a man with a steady job and a good salary, but, you know.'

'I cannot believe you. You're being such a bitch.'

'Well, I pay for everything when I am with you and Scar.'

This stings me. How dare she?

'You always insist on paying for everything, or just do it.'

'You never stop me.'

Any other time I would think about this and be rational but she is being such a bitch.

'I live in a shitty house share and have worked every shitty job you can think of. I have always paid my way my entire life. You on the other hand were given a property and have never worked a day in your entire life.'

I can tell from her face that was a bullseye. We stare at each other with burning rage. Then I pick up all my stuff and leave. I have no idea what got into her but there is nothing more to say.

When I walk out of her house it is raining. Life will always get worse just when you think you cannot take any more, and you just absorb it.

My limbs are shaking from our argument. I should have known that her insistence of paying for everything was not genuine. That it would leave a stain on our friendship. I feel guilty but it is lessened by her sexist comments. I would expect them from anyone, but Claudia?

I don't know where I am going but I keep walking, and I get soaked. I take my phone out and look at the time. Six o'clock. I had no idea it was so late. William's game must be over. I wonder if he is having a drink with friends. I miss him, but not because I had an argument with Claudia. I miss him in an aching way. All the time. I miss him when I am not with him. He is my first thought in the morning and last thought at night.

I have spent my life solely focused on my career and, just like that, it is no longer enough. If I have truly fallen out with Claudia, then William is all I have left.

Family is important when your family live hundreds of miles away. You know you have to build your own tribe from scratch. Choose the right people carefully. Ones that will not damage your heart too much. I call William. He is my family. He is the only roots I have, securing me to the ground and letting me know I am loved.

He picks up on the first ring.

'Hello, you.'

'Hello, how did the game go?'

'It went well. How is your evening with Claudia going? She pissed yet?'

'Pissed off, more like.'

'What?'

'We had a massive fight.'

'Oh no, what about.'

'You, actually.'

William laughs. 'Uh *oh, what did I do?*'

'She called me a gold digger.'

I can hear William splutter on the other end.

'Well, that was a dick move.'

'Indeed.'

'I don't want you to worry. We both know that's not true.'

'Thank you. That makes me feel better.'

'Tell you what, come to me. We can get a takeaway and get into bed.'

'That sounds amazing. I'm on my way.'

'Wonderful, see you soon. Love you.'

I stop walking and feel like I have been hit with the kindest blow. This is not the first time he has said the L word, but hearing it still makes me feel giddy.

'I love you too. I really do.'

'I'll see you soon. You're amazing.'

'You too, see you soon.'

I head to the tube and manage to get a seat. I get there before William but he is not far behind. When I see him my heart leaps. I am falling further and further in and I am not scared about it any more. I practically run to him and we kiss. It fills me up, makes me happy. He carries me up the stairs and swiftly unlocks the door with one hand.

As soon as we are through the door, I am pawing at his clothes. We have quick and passionate sex on the stairs.

'Tash.'

'Yes, my love.'

William lifts his head from my shoulder and looks into my eyes. He pushes the hair from my face and kisses me.

'I love you.'

'I love you, too.'

Then he gets on one knee and pulls a box out of his pocket. I gasp. Everything becomes strange and surreal. He opens the box and there is, indeed, a ring in it. I cannot believe this is happening.

'Tash, I know we have only been together for a year but I love you. You're everything to me. You have made my life so much better. Will you marry me?'

'Yes, yes, I will marry you. Oh my God, I'm so happy!'

He places the ring on my finger and I let out a little scream. It is a gold ring with a huge sapphire in the middle and lots of little diamonds around it. It is beautiful. I try to bottle this moment. The pure joy of it. I am going to marry my best friend.

Three weeks pass before Claudia sends me a message. It is not a sorry, it is some random video of a cat hitting a printer. There is a funny subtitle over it. I laugh. The cat does look like it is annoyed the printer won't work. I don't reply straight away. If she wants to resume our friendship, she can do it in a way which is not so antisocial. Like, with an actual apology.

In the end my conscious gets the better of me and I reply with a laughing emoji. Nothing else. I will not ignore her but that is it. Three hours later she calls me.

'Hi,' she says. It sounds like she is forcing the words out.

'Hi,' I reply. I am forcing the words out too.

Then there is a pause. A long one. We are both putting our pride before our friendship. The realisation smarts at me. We have been friends for five years now. That means more than my ego.

'I'm sorry you pay for everything. We'll make sure it doesn't happen in the future.'

'Thank you, but you're right. I always aggressively insist on paying for everything. That's my own thing.'

'I didn't mean what I said.'

'Neither did I. I'm sorry. You're my best friend. I love you, Tash.'

'I love you too, Claud.'

'So, can we make up? I miss you.'

'Of course, don't be silly. Nothing and no one will ever come between us. We are friends forever.'

'Can we meet up tonight?'

'Sorry, I'm already doing something with William.'

'Oh, okay.' Her disappointment is palpable. I feel a brief moment of guilt but I do not want to miss an evening with William. Our time together is so precious. I do not want to let him down.

*'We're having a party soon.'*

*'We?'*

*'William and I.'*

*'Oh.'*

I guess I should tell her now. Rip off the plaster but something stops me. I don't want my happiness to hurt her.

*'What is it?'*

I stay silent. Wondering if I should tell her.

*'I know you're holding something back, tell me what it is.'*

*'We're engaged.'*

I can hear a sharp inhale of breath on the other end but she composes herself quickly.

*'That's amazing. I'm happy for you.'*

*'The party is an engagement party.'*

*'Wow! That is so fab. I cannot wait. Send me all the details.'*

*'I will.'*

*'See each other soon?'*

*'Super soon. We will fix a date ASAP.'*

*'Ya!'*

With that Claudia hangs up. I am glad we are friends again, but I know it will take a while for the scars to heal.

Claudia is the first person to arrive at the engagement party. She arrives with a box from Tiffany's. I wish she hadn't. Maybe when you are born into money in a world where most people struggle financially, being generous is your power. She looks stunning. She is in an off-the-shoulder black dress and silver, strappy high heels. Jimmy Choo probably. Her blond hair is natural, unlike mine and is voluptuous and wavy. She has the smallest, pertest nose I have ever seen. She really is a sight to behold. If I were a man, or gay, I would throw myself at her feet.

'You're smiling.'

'Of course, I am. You're here. I have missed you.'

She arches an eyebrow at me. We have not seen each other in the run up to the party. William and I have been in the cosiest love bubble. Neither of us have wanted to go and see other people. I am ashamed to realise I have become one of those women who just dump their female friends when a man comes along.

'Are you free at any point next week?'

Claudia perks up at this. A smile crosses her face and I can even see a little tear in her eye. I feel awful.

'Oh, Claud.' I wrap my arms around her and give her a big squeeze. 'I'm sorry we didn't see each other for ages. I promise I will be better. It's me and you against the world. We're going to be friends forever.'

At this point Claudia starts to sniffle but stops herself. Claudia is proper and would never ruin anyone's engagement party by making it all about her.

'Do you promise me? Because you will probably be knocked up soon and then we will never see each other again.'

'I promise. We will always be friends and I will always make time for you.' I mean it and I make the promise to myself. There is a worry there too because what

Claudia does not know is that I already am knocked up and a part of me fears she is right.

# Chapter 21

## Now

I look out of the window, a cup of tea in hand. I look at the beautiful trees and plants in our garden. The gardener really knows his stuff. The sky is the lightest grey and the clouds gather and rain down on us. It is beautiful. There is something special about being inside when it is raining outside. I can hear the *tap tap* on our skylights and watch as more raindrops hit the puddles, calming me. I need that.

The meeting has put a rage in me. Who the hell do they think they are? I had my first acting job when I was fifteen. A tiny little role I got as a fluke. Some casting directors came to our school and I got the part out of hundreds of other children. It lit a fire in me and I have worked for two decades making a career for myself. For a lot of that time, I was out of work or studying but I have always had my eyes on the prize.

I have sacrificed everything for my career. Friends, family events, a social life. I missed both of my children's first steps. I have made hundreds of millions for the film industry and I have won an Oscar. Yet they still speak to me as if I am a little girl. A stupid little girl.

I think back to all the times I was forced to do something I did not want to do. When my voice seemed to leave me and my body shut down because some jerk had his hands on my bottom or copped a feel of my breast. No one watches female lead films? They are the ones who are stupid.

I talked to Claudia once about an idea I had. It was a dream about a collective. Actors coming together to share information and make movies together. This is what our production company will be. A safe place for all actors, writers, producers and directors. There will be no harassment, bullying or abuse. Women will have an equal place and so will black and Asian actors. Sam Cooke was right, 'A Change is Gonna Come.' It starts now. I will call it Phoenix productions because we will rise from the ashes of the corrupt industry that has hurt us for so long.

The air is biting as I step out into the darkness. It is four in the morning and my driver is here. I walk to the car and get in. The nervousness feels like a sickness. There is bile in my throat. Today is the first day of my directorial debut. We found the perfect book and bought the film rights. We found the investors and hired everybody. There are parts for Claudia, Scarlet and me. This will be a colossal mistake or a resounding success. But if it is a mistake, then I tried and I will have learnt a lot.

It is a big world out there and I am married with two children. If I crash and burn, it is not the end of the world. I take the call sheet out of my bag. It is easy enough. I have acted in thirty-one films in my career. I can do this. I know how. Better, still, I have no scenes today. No make-up, no costume. I am just the director and I can focus on the story without my own ego coming into play. My outfit of jeans, *Uggs*, a T-shirt, a jumper and a coat is comfy and feels like a protective shield.

We arrive at the location quickly. There is not a lot of traffic at this time. I get out of the car and thank the driver. I head in and greet everyone. They are all looking at me with awe.

'Right, let's make some tea and coffee. Warm up those bones.'

An assistant jumps up.

'I will make the tea and coffee and put the biscuits out.'

I am about to tell her I will make my own but I stop. It is her job and I do not want to try too hard.

A smile breaks out onto my face and stays there for the rest of the day. When the first shot is set up and I call 'action' for the first time I feel a rush of power. I am part of the change now and this is just the start.

We break for lunch and we all eat together. I refuse to have a hierarchy on my film set. The film industry is all about hierarchy. The entire world is about hierarchy. One big ladder we are all trying to climb. Some of us never stood a chance. We were born at the bottom and we stay there. We were not blessed with intelligence or looks or by the lucky sperm club. We did not come from money and have no secure base. Others are born at the top and are terrible people. Others look like they have everything but their lives are lonely or full of tragedy.

To be born into a warm and loving family is, to me, the greatest wealth of all. I did not have that but William did. But I had confidence anyway. I have no idea where it came from. I have always known I was destined for greatness and that I would make something of my life. All of this, despite not being born into money or having any support. I come from nothing, absolutely nothing. Yet here I am against all the odds. I try to think what would have happened if I had not won that scholarship to RADA. An extraordinary moment of luck that started my career. No, started my entire life.

Not everyone gets that moment of extraordinary luck. I wonder how many working-class actors out there become successful. The industry is full of Cambridge and Oxford graduates. It is a middle-class and privileged industry, full of posh accents and the children of famous people. Most people have a relative in the industry, never mind how it expects so many to work for free for years. The injustice bites at me. I have lived my life thinking if I can do it anyone can, but now I am not so sure.

I look around the set and I start to wonder how many of these people come from a home that is well off but has no love, or has no money and a fantastic support system. Privilege is not an obvious thing. It is something that separates us in various ways. It pulls us apart from each other just as our differences do. Life is hard for everyone, I know that. There is always more than meets the eye.

I make a promise to myself that I will always hire with diversity in mind and not with shallow thinking.

Claudia, Scarlet and I all go to the cinema at the weekend. We watch a film called Bridesmaids. It is a female lead film. Everyone is talking about it. The media, the industry. They are all saying the R word and they are right. I can feel it in the air. Viva la revolution.

The next day I get a call from Giles and Myles. They want to know if I have anything like Bridesmaids because it is a 'trend' they want to get involved in. I give a polite no by telling them I am too busy at the moment to work with them or send projects their way. They are surprised, I can tell. Powerful men are not used to hearing no. People rarely say no to them.

Then there is a rumbling about James Hervey. Some people are saying journalists are asking questions and I start to think about the wisdom of Sam Cooke all over again.


Our film wins the biggest award at Sundance. Just like that I am an actor-director. I do a million interviews and they all ask me if I did this because I am an actress who is almost forty and am I scared that I am almost forty. Unless they are asking me about my lipstick or what designers I wear. No one asks men these questions. Of course they don't. Men are not constantly made to feel as if they have to worship at the God of superficiality. But, hey, if women are busy making themselves look as fuckable as possible, then they do not have time to work on their brains, work hard and take over the world. It is oppression at its best. Unless you open your eyes, you cannot tell you are being oppressed at all. Then when you talk, people get defensive. They want things to be the same. They want you to be quiet. They resist you, they ignore you but then the change comes. If you work hard enough and do not back down. Then you make the world a better place.

# Chapter 22

## Now

Scarlet looks different on FaceTime today. Slightly, dare I say it, plumper. Considering how thin she was before this it can only be a good thing. She looked like a two-year-old at one point. I am trying not to ask her how things are going with Alex. I know I am married and it is none of my business but my crush on Alex has made me feel, rightly or wrongly, that I have some kind of claim on him. That Scarlet is having sex with him makes me jealous. I feel ashamed but I cannot help it. I even fantasise about him. It makes me feel like I am cheating on William but I am sure he does the same. There is nothing wrong with some casual window shopping, is there?

'So, I have been working as an assistant producer and it is, like, so enlightening.'

Scarlet has started using the term "like" as punctuation. She is a proper Angeleno now; skinny, healthy, enlightened, a ruthless operator dressed up as a zen hippy.

'Really? How so?'

'Well, I've been helping with casting for this one thing. It is good for an actor so see the other side. We cast a music video and the women who came in just flirted with the guys and were really sexual with them. The guys were just lapping it up and encouraging them. It was like I was invisible. One of the models, who looked nothing like her picture at all, I mean you would have to take off ten years and twenty pounds, was like, "You are a producer? You?"' She kept saying it over and over. All the women were like that, they were either hugely dismissive or just ignored me completely. I guess they think their powers have no effect on me as I am a woman and their best bet was making the men hard.'

'That's so depressing, Scar. Didn't that producer we met in Cannes refer to model slash actresses as mattresses because of what they'll do to get the part?'

Scarlet laughs but I do not find it funny. I find it disgusting and inappropriate that I work in an industry where you can fuck yourself to success.

'It's not funny, Scar. It's awful and depressing.'

Scarlet is still laughing. She is in stitches.

'They must be upset you do not swing that way.'

Scarlet has finally stopped laughing and looks at me. 'No one swings anyway, Tash, you don't fall in love with someone because of their genitals. It's about who they are as a person.'

'What? Is there something you want to tell me?'

'There is no such thing as gender.'

'Okay,' I say.

'I have had affairs with a lot of beautiful people. This one yoga instructor was perfect. She had the most gorgeous breasts and a perfect bottom.'

I try to not let my jaw hit the floor. Wow! I had no idea. I feel old fashioned and boring. My life feels so pedestrian compared to Scarlet's.

'Jesus, Tash, remove your jaw from the floor. You look like you have never lived.'

I close my mouth and feel self-conscious.

'Well good for you, all these different experiences are good.'

'Yes, they were,' she says with a deep, long sigh. I would not want to read her mind right now.

'The casting couch is not okay.'

'Oh, Tash, I agree. Not that a prude like you would sleep on it anyway. You would never have made it.'

'Well, I guess that's true. You don't need to sleep on the casting couch to make it. I mean, most people don't, I reckon, but they tend to make you do loads of nudity.'

'But who minds that? We all look the same. A naked body is a naked body.'

I get her point but I do not think it is as simple as that.

'So how is Alex?'

I try to make it sound casual.

'Huh?' she says, she is day dreaming and barely listening.

'Alex, your boyfriend.'

'Oh, yes, well I would not call him that exactly but we had a wonderful threesome last night with a French actress that we both know. She is only in town for one more day.'

Christ. I think Alex might be in a different sphere from me after all. There is a long silence that follows. It is uncomfortable, at least on my end.

'That sounds…' I cannot think of a word. 'Nice.'

Scarlet laughs again.

'You're so funny, Tash. With your suburban life and your kids and your lawyer husband. It's like you're not an artist at all.'

The comment bites at me. What is wrong with being grounded and married?

'Someone's marital and parental status hardly has an effect on their ability to act, Scar, and ditto for where I live.'

'Okay, okay, don't get your knickers in a twist. I am just saying you should be freer and explore more.'

'Well, with all due respect, you have no idea what the fuck you're talking about. Thanks for filling me in with everything. We'll speak soon.'

With this I hang up. I know I should not have reacted but who does she think she is? I am a better actress than she is ever going to be. You do not have to fuck around all the time to be good at art.

The anger gives me a massive rush of energy that has to go somewhere. I head to our home gym and do a HIIT workout followed by some yoga. Then I shower with everything that involves; body brushing, soap, exfoliate, scalp exfoliate, hair mask, shampoo and conditioner. Then I dry off and moisturise all over. I add various serums to my face and use my *creme de la mer*. The upkeep to look like this is exhausting but I have to keep the size fourteen with thighs that rub as she walks and frizzy hair at bay. It is not that no one would hire that woman, but she would never be a movie star.

Two and a half hours later I head into the living room to read scripts. The children are at a sleep over and the house feels empty. William is at a work event but I hope he will be home soon. We do not get a lot of alone time and this would be the perfect opportunity to spend a nice evening together.

The script is awful and has a woman being raped on page twenty. How is that entertainment? Disgusted, I put it down. I log into my social media accounts. Most actors have someone to do this for them and I am no different, but I also do it myself. I want to be authentic but to come across as authentic you have to be a little fake.

I go into the bathroom and put a little make-up on and then I take a selfie on my phone. I know all about lighting and angles and I have the perfect no make-up, natural selfie after twenty attempts. I place the perfect filter on it and upload it to my Instagram account. My Instagram account is linked to my Twitter and my Facebook Fan page. All roads lead to the one thing. I have to make sure I am current and on trend. Casting directors now hire people according to how many followers they have on their various social media accounts. This is a 24/7 job. I do not think people realise just how much work goes into it. You have to always be on. Well, unless you are asleep.

*Just at home chilling. Had a nice bath and reading some scripts. How do you guys relax? Xxx*

It gets loads of likes instantly. I feel happy, the part of my brain that craves the attention lights up like a firework. Ego stroked. Scarlet sends a message.

*See, I love you, but you are a basic bitch.*

*Whatever, darling, it is my USP and ONE of us is a movie star*, I reply.

She does not reply to that. Of course she doesn't, because I actually have a career and she is a bit part actress. I hate it when I am bitchy and smug but I fully embrace the feeling. Fuck her, fuck everyone. I am a star!

*Then*

I drink tea in the kitchen of my house share. The kitchen is one of the better rooms. Probably the second best one after the living room with its television and sofa. The television in my room is tiny in comparison. I would rectify that, but now I am pregnant William and I are going to move in together. William lives in a flat share at the moment so we need to find somewhere together. I have terrible morning sickness and I am throwing up five times a day.

The sink is full of dirty dishes and so is the top of the washing machine and the kitchen top. The cleaner comes once a week. I try to remember the day. How could I have lived here for years and not know what day the cleaner comes? From the hardened food on the dishes that have been there for ages, she must be coming soon.

Distractions are everything at the moment. The auditions have come in. The big ones. I auditioned for a Nicole Kidman movie two weeks ago. Then another one with Steven Spielberg. The one I am waiting to hear from now is for the lead part in the biggest book of the year. They have auditioned thousands of actresses and I am down to the last two. If I get this, my life will change completely. If I don't, I will still be a middling, bit part actress. I still feel the fear that I will never make it. I have almost run out of money. If I do not get acting work soon, I will have to get a crappy job again. I was so happy when I had a year's worth of rent money in my bank account. Funny how it runs down so fast.

I had a screaming argument with a girl who lives with me yesterday. I find her nosy and too much, but I am full of guilt today. She makes bitchy comments about William coming over too much or me taking too long in the shower. She isn't that bad really. Maybe I feel kinder as this has all become temporary. Still, the thought that I will run out of money and have to rely on William after I have the baby terrifies me.

I keep going over to my phone. I have been trying to ignore it and keep myself busy. I have rearranged, cleaned, and organised everything in my room. I have exercised and completed my full beauty routine and it is still only four in the afternoon.

I am about to break and just do everyone's dishes when the phone rings. I have never run so fast in my life. I answer it. It is my agent.

'Hi, Louise, did I get it?'

'You got it. The part is yours.'

I have to hold onto the kitchen counter to balance myself. The nausea makes me throw up in my mouth a little. I got the part.

I thank Louise and then hang up the phone. I will not be doing the dishes after all.

My life is never going to be the same again.

'Hi, Natasha.'

I jump. It is Christina. A house mate that has made my life hell every chance she gets. Luckily, I am rarely home so I hardly ever see her, but when I do there is always a chorus of bitchy comments. They never stop. She always blames the dishes on me too, even though, I always wash mine. I once heard her tell our fellow housemates that I was anorexic.

I think about whether I should tell her my good news but it would taint it. I find most people do not like it when extraordinary things happen to other people. It brings out the worst in them. I smile at her instead. I want to keep this exquisite secret to myself. There is only one person I want to tell and I am meeting him later today. I cannot wait.

William looks ecstatic when I tell him but then I see something else. It looks like fear. That happens when you start to become successful, people start to worry that you are going to leave them behind. Or they start to resent you. I wonder if my relationship with William will be another casualty of wanting more in life. I take his hand and stroke it, trying to allay his fears. He smiles back but the worry remains. I am glad our baby is growing in my tummy and his ring is on my finger. It makes us solid.

'That's the role of a lifetime. Well done, Tash.'

'Well, hopefully not. Fingers crossed; it's just the start.'

'Where are you filming?'

'Canada. For three months.'

He flinches and now it is my time to worry. What if our relationship does not last? I love him. Will I have to choose?

'What about the baby?'

'What do you mean?'

'You're pregnant. Maybe you should take it easy.'

'I'm not ill, just pregnant. Pregnant women work all the time.'

He does not look convinced. I feel upset but I bury it. I have to leave next week and I want our time together to be perfect.

'I'm only six weeks. I'll be back in plenty of time before the birth.'

He doesn't look convinced.

'What if something goes wrong?'

'They have doctors in Canada.'

'But I won't be there. If something goes wrong you will be on your own.'

'Don't be so doom and gloom. Why would something go wrong?'

William's brow becomes furrowed. I can tell he is not convinced. Still, he tries to pretend. He lifts his glass.

'To my darling Natasha. She will soon be the biggest superstar in the world.'

I laugh and clink glasses with him and we toast. This is one of the happiest moments of my entire life but there is an undercurrent that ebbs and flows. I do not think I am lucky enough to have it all.

'Did you tell them you're pregnant?'

'No.'

'Don't you think you should?'

'They might replace me.'

'There might be a legal issue.'

The thought of this worries me. Could they sue me? Or fire me? Again, I feel angry. Everything has become tainted. The joy is no longer unencumbered. All I wanted was this moment but now it is gone. There is a lull. A moment of sadness as we both lick our wounds. I can tell he is not happy. What did he think was going to happen? I would get pregnant and marry and give up my career?

'When are we going to tell people about the baby?' He asks me.

'I think twelve weeks is standard.'

'My mother's going to be happy. She's always wanted a grandchild. She's going to be an amazing grandmother.'

'I'm sure, she will.'

'Anyway, I have a surprise.'

I am taken aback. William is not spontaneous.

'Oh.'

'I will show you after lunch. It's exciting.'

After lunch, we walk through London hand-in-hand. We take it in. I love this city. It is full of beauty. I leapt into its arms with all the courage that I had and it paid off in droves. William stops abruptly in front of a beautiful house we had viewed previously on a whim. It was out of our budget but we wanted to see what was out there, have a moment to live our dream life. William looks at me. I look back at him.

'What is this?'

'What do you think this is?'

'Have you rented this because I thought it was for sale?'

'I haven't rented it.'

I look at him. Shocked. We had both been putting money into a joint account for a deposit but I had to stop this month. I am sure there is not enough money in there for this house.

'It's ours, Tash. My parents gave me a loan and we had our money. It's not agreed yet, but they accepted the offer and they want a quick exchange. The mortgage will be huge but...'

Before William can finish his sentence, I kiss him. I am so happy.

'Yes, yes, a million times. Let's do it. Let's build a life in this beautiful house.'

William does a little fist pump and then kisses me back. Turns out this day was fixable after all. The bricks and mortar, the baby, the ring. Finally, it sinks in. This is forever. William is the father of my child and we will be married soon. He is not going to leave me.

When I arrive in Canada, I do fourteen-hour days, six days a week. I rang to tell my agent that I was pregnant before I left for Canada. I could tell she was pissed but the producers came back saying the director had fallen in love with me and could not imagine anyone else in the role. It reminded me that one of my drama teachers had told me that someone, somewhere, would fall in love with you eventually and then that would start your career. You just had to keep the faith.

It was a lot better than the other drama teachers who always told us ninety per cent of us would be out of work at any one time. I think about that a lot. Apart from Claudia and Scarlet I have only seen one other person I knew at RADA on the television. It was for a commercial. No one else seems to have made it other than me, Claudia and Scarlet.

I spend most of Sunday Skyping William. We write each other long emails and send endless pictures. Some of them sexy, some of them not. I worry about all the beautiful women that always seem to throw themselves at him.

We have a sexy Skype session where I show him exactly what he is missing. I take all my clothes off and spread my legs for the camera. It has the desired effect. He is naked in no time and he comes quickly when he masturbates. So do I. We do this at least once a week. I wonder if this is enough or if I am just riling him up for another woman.

I wonder what I would do if he cheated on me. Cheating is rife in the film industry. I guess it makes sense, you spend so long with the other actor and you usually see each other naked. Being away for months on end puts you in a bubble. You become so separated from your real life and your family. Everyone gets lonely, but I refuse. I know my father cheated on my mother when he was in the military. She forgave him each time. She said that men and women have different sex drives. That always pissed me off. Women like sex just as much as men.

I skype with Claudia but I have not told her about my pregnancy yet. I promised myself after the engagement party that I would never fail her as a friend again. She is like my sister. I love Claudia.

I wait in my trailer as they set up the next shot. It is the ultimate in luxury and is much bigger than the room I rent in London. I take a picture and send it to William. He responds quickly.

*Looks amazing, darling. I would expect nothing less. Xx*

The weeks have passed quickly and I will be home soon. I am not showing, thankfully. There were a lot of meetings about how they would hide my bump but they have not needed to. There are only two-and-a-half weeks left so I am not sure I will have to carry any of the big bags they bought to place in front of my bump, like Grace Kelly.

The AD comes to get me for the scene. Thank God. I was getting bored. The film industry is all hurry up and wait. I send William a text back.

*Not even close to how amazing our home is. Time has gone fast. See you soon. Miss you, my love. xxx*

I head to set. It is time for action.

I do a ton of press for the film. I find it hilarious that any of the journalists will even know who I am. Every single paper and magazine I have ever heard of interviews me. Every journalist asks me what it feels like that I am about to become famous. The question is incomprehensible. I have no idea what it is like to be famous and I am not sure I want to be. I want to make movies and be successful but do I want everyone in the world to know who I am? I thought I did but now I am not so sure. It feels scary.

The press comes out before we even finish filming. I get calls and emails from everyone I have ever met. My Facebook is full of friend requests. My agent recommends a publicist and I hire her. The publicist recommends a stylist and I hire her. Soon I have a team. Everyone tells me I am a movie star, even though the film has not come out yet. Everyone is so nice to me. People start to set up meetings. I still have to audition sometimes but I start to get straight offers. My life has completely changed. It is everything I ever wanted. So why am I so terrified?

# Chapter 23

## Now

I can hear the phone ringing. I only hope it is William's phone. I am not ready to get up. My sleep is as broken as ever. Both children got me up numerous times. William sleeps like the dead. He always has been like that.

I nudge him, hard. He grunts but does not wake up. I kick him. Hard. There is a bit of movement and fumbling. He reaches for his phone clumsily without opening his eyes. He lifts it up and gives it a glance.

'Not me.'

I groan but then the ringing stops. I am relieved but then I'm worried about why someone would be calling so early. I sit up, awake now. Fuck's sake. I am so tired my eyes hurt. I reach for my phone. It is Claudia. A moment of complete panic engulfs me. I call her back.

'Tash!'

'Are you okay?'

'What? Of course, I am.'

'What time is it?' I ask, not trying to hide how pissed off I am.

'How can you not have heard?'

I look at the time on my phone. Six a.m. What the fuck?

'It is six in the morning, Claud. No one has heard anything at this time. Anyone with any luck is asleep.'

'It's James Hervey.'

That gets me up.

'Oh no, Claudia, did he hurt you? That bastard!'

'Oh, Tash, don't be silly. James Hervey knows the family I come from. He knows my dad would probably hire a Mossad agent to rip his bloody balls off.'

'Then what.'

'He has been arrested!'

'Wow! That's amazing.' A feeling comes over me. It is complete joy. Everywhere I look I see men who have been accused of sexual assault in positions of power. I have never heard of a powerful man having to face the consequences of his actions against women. Today feels like a new day.

'Are you feeling it too?'

'I am.'

'It is a new world, Tash. This is just the beginning.'

She is right. I can feel it in my bones.

I look at the BBC news on my phone. It is everywhere. I go onto Facebook and Twitter. It is all everyone is talking about and there is something else too, a hashtag that people are using to raise awareness and make people accountable. A hashtag that is from an older social movement that is needed now more than ever. It is small but powerful; #metoo.

# Chapter 24

## Now

There are more champagne bottles than I can count. They fill up the entire pantry. Everywhere there are people buzzing about. The party planner Yolanda has really outdone herself. The garden is full of fairy lights. Waiters bustle around, pouring champagne and making cocktails. The canapés look delicious. I insisted on having some mini burgers. I want to gobble them all up right now. Later there will be fireworks.

Today will be magnificent because it has to be. It is my fortieth birthday. The number scares me. I cannot deny I am middle-aged now. A forty-year-old actress. An endangered species. I try to not think about it. I want to enjoy this evening.

I look out of the window. There are a lot of paparazzi. I may still be relevant after all. I look at the various dresses sprawled out on the bed. A number of designers have sent me clothes. I am sample size so they like me. If you are not sample size, they tend to just send icy judgement in your direction instead. Clothes are for thin people only, apparently.

I put all fears of career failure aside. I have invited everyone who is anyone to this party. Claudia will be here and Scarlet too. The children have spent months planning their outfits. I spent what felt like days online shopping with Amelia. There is such a change in a girl when they reach double figures. They grow up so quickly. It is terrifying. I still cannot believe that Joseph is a teenager now. It all happened so quickly. I am half way through my life. It feels like death is already knocking on my door.

I decide on the bright pink dress. All I want in my life is joy and brightness. I add some gold Jimmy Choo strappy sandals. I go to my jewellery box. Tonight needs all the bling. I pick each piece up carefully, taking my time to make my choice. I am a lucky woman. There are a lot of beautiful pieces here. William has always been generous. I pick up a chunky white-gold ring which has seventy-five diamonds. Two rows of normal diamonds and two of champagne diamonds. It is just the kind of glitz tonight calls for. I also see my favourite piece; my Cartier panther bracelet. It is a gorgeous piece and is so striking with its green-emerald eyes. I remember when I bought it. I had just made my first big pay check. William and I had a fight and after he left for a walk to cool down, I took myself to New Bond Street. I was a wealthy woman in my own right. I felt powerful. I saw the piece in a magazine, Vogue, I think it was, and I decided that I had to have it. It cost six figures. It was one of the most exhilarating moments of my life. My move into becoming the person I am now. Every time I look at it, I feel nothing but pride. I could tell William was upset when he saw it. Emasculated probably. The timing would not have helped. But I was sick of apologising for my success. Sick of making myself less. I am not less. I have become everything I was ever going to be. It takes true courage to reach your full potential. I am not finished yet. I put the bracelet on. The knee-length halter neck dress does not need a necklace. I look in the mirror. Perfect.

I walk down the stairs and the first thing I see is William in his tux. He gives a long, slow whistle.

'What a stunner. I'm a lucky man indeed.' He reaches out for my hand and I give it to him. He kisses it.

'You're such a romantic. I love it.'

He gives me a smile. We are still together. So much has been thrown at us and we are still in love. I feel lucky every day. We decided to be honest to each other after my crush on Alex and his kiss with Claire. Now we make sure that if one of us is working, the other isn't. We sleep in the same bed every night. I turned down another movie with Alex because it had sex scenes. We have worked hard on our marriage and it has paid off.

He notices the bracelet and his smile reaches his eyes. I see those crinkles that I love.

'I'm so proud to be married to a woman who can buy her own jewellery.'

'Thank you.' I kiss him.

'I will give you your present later. I cannot promise it will rival your cat.' He laughs.

'I will love it more.'

We head into the garden. This moment always makes me nervous. When you do not know who is going to turn up. Or if anyone is. My social anxiety is off the scale. Then I see my fellow blond. Claudia. My sister from another mother. I let out a girly scream. Claudia joins in and William covers his ears.

'*Jeez,* why do women do that? My ears are ringing.'

I squeeze Claudia so hard that I might break her. I want to soak her up.

'Jesus, can you believe we are forty?' I ask her.

'Can you believe we have known each other for over twenty years?'

My mouth hangs open. 'That cannot be true.'

'And yet it is.'

'Christ. I feel ancient.'

'That is because you are, darling.'

'*Touché!*'

We both start laughing. The waiter comes over with a tray of champagne. We all take a glass.

'To my beautiful Natasha on her birthday. She is as beautiful as ever.'

Claudia and I go 'aw' and we all toast.

'Where are the kids?'

'Somewhere in the house. They are,' I try to think of an appropriate word. 'A force.'

Claudia laughs. She knows. She is their godmother after all.

'Is his Lordship coming?'

'No, he couldn't do today. I think he has something with Wills and Kate.'

Claudia married someone titled a few years back. He is ten years older than her and is rich beyond measure. He owns half of Britain. She is the lady of the manor now and loves it. She doesn't act any more. Apparently, the aristocracy think it is beneath them. Court jesters or something. But Claudia and I still produce. She leaves the acting to me.

'What about the twins?'

'With the nannies.'

She has an army of them and no qualms about using them. Lucky bitch.

'Is Scarlet coming?'

'Yes. She RSVP'd anyway.'

'I doubt she would miss a social event like this. It is all everyone is talking about.'

I feel excited. Not bad for a working-class Scot; becoming the talking point of the chattering classes.

'Is she coming with Alex?' William asks, looking at me. I can't see any jealousy. I hope Alex has lost his power over him.

'No, they got divorced, remember? They share custody of Bear,

I see it click. 'Oh yes, I remember seeing that on the cover of some tabloid. Quickie Las Vegas wedding, even quicker divorce. Managed to pop out a child in the middle of it,' William says with amusement in his voice. He tends to avoid Scarlet. They have never liked each other. Scarlet is half hippie, half Machiavelli. She worships two gods; Buddha and fame. Scarlet and Alex made William and I godparents. Claudia too, and some powerful movers and shakers. Half friends, half people who could advance careers. I can't help but admire Scarlet. I am ambitious and ruthless too; it is the only way to become a movie star but she does not even try to hide it. Her ruthless ambition is as naked as it comes.

I notice Claudia has only taken the merest sip of her champagne and I am about to say something but then the throngs arrive. A sea of people all at once. Lots of famous faces, powerful editors, producers, directors; the lot. I take a deep breath. Here we go.

First up is the editor of Stylish magazine. The leading fashion magazine. This woman probably has more power than the Prime Minister. She is certainly more talented and connected.

'What a gorgeous dress, darling. We always love your style. We must do a piece on you. It has been too long.'

I try to ignore the giddy feeling in my stomach. I am not a teenage girl. Do not be grateful or starstruck, I tell myself. You are their equal. They are lucky to have you.

'Darling, I would love that. I read the magazine every month. It would be an honour.'

She kisses me on both cheeks and then moves on to where the champagne is flowing, two assistants and her husband in tow. Now there is a woman I can respect.

Producers and directors offer me work and I have wonderful conversations with actors I have worked with. I have few friends but a lot of acquaintances. This is not a diss on my acquaintances. They do not mean less to me. I love them just as much. I just do not share my personal life with them. Considering how indiscreet most of them are, this is a good thing.

I look back at William and Claudia to make sure they are okay. William is talking to Ian McEwan. He looks a bit like an excited schoolboy. He loves his books. Claudia is talking to the editor of Stylish. I think she interned for her at one point, before she decided on drama school. I imagine it was much like The Devil Wears Prada.

I walk around the party, saying hi to people and making general chit-chat. I want to have a moment with every single person here. It dawns on me that I could have done something more relaxing for my birthday but staying on top is a twenty-four/seven job. We have the entire weekend to have family fun. That is when the real celebration will begin.

'Can you believe he went to jail?' They are talking about James Hervey. He got twenty-one years for rape and sexual assault. We all celebrated that day. My female friends and I all met up for a champagne lunch to toast the bastard. Justice is rare but sweet when it comes.

I can see my children near the Pimms bar. They better be drinking a virgin one. They are on strict instructions to behave. They can let their hair down tomorrow. They both look gorgeous and so tall all of a sudden. They have grown up so much in the last few months.

Patrick Mulligan is taking pictures. He is one of the biggest photographers there is. He works for *Vogue* and *Vanity Fair* all the time. All the guests will get a photo book to remind them of tonight.

My family is here. They always whine when I invite them to things like this, saying it is 'not their world' and make a big deal about not coming. In the end, they do. I am happy they are here. Our relationship is better now we live so far away from each other. Distance really does make the heart grow fonder. I talk to them all the time now, and we FaceTime with the children at least once a week. We stopped batting our resentments at each other and chose kindness instead.

The biggest band of the moment will be performing soon. I feel happy and proud. I am like Irving Thalberg as I walk around my huge garden and look back at my big, beautiful house. 'I own this, I own this. I own all of this.'

Well done, Natasha. You did good.

*Tatler*, *Vogue*, *Vanity Fair* and *Stylish* have all asked to run the pictures from the party and most of the papers already have. It is also online and it made the news. And those are the outlets that I saw. Overall, it was a resounding success. Offers of work have come pouring in and I can't think of a better PR stunt.

William has a terrible hangover the next day so I try to make breakfast. He refuses, saying it is my birthday weekend. He makes pancakes with blueberries, maple syrup and whipped cream. There is coffee on the side. The kitchen island is overflowing with deliciousness. I sit on one of our vintage stools and flip through the newspapers while indulging in breakfast heaven.

The sound of creaking floorboards lets me know the children are awake. They come down the stairs with their slouchy, lazy, too-cool-for-anything demeanour. My heart leaps in my chest. It never gets old, having children. They do something to excite me every day.

'Hi, Mum, great party.' Joseph kisses me on the cheek. 'I met Jimmy Page. It was the best thing ever. I love old bands.'

Ah yes, Joseph is going through his old legends phase. All I hear coming out of his room is Led Zeppelin and the Rolling Stones. Amelia on the other hand is into Motown. She loves rhythm and blues and soul singers. Though, some of the ones she calls 'old' are the ones I grew up with. My mortality is everywhere now I have hit the big four-o. Amelia loves a bit of Beyonce, too. My children have great taste.

I can hear more movement in the house. Claudia and Scarlet must be up. They both ended up staying. Alex did not turn up, he ended up on babysitting duties, Scarlet said. I can't help thinking there is more to the story. Maybe they had a fight.

Claudia comes down the stairs first. Her hair looks like a bird's nest and you can tell she is battling a killer hangover. Her face has the perfect expression of someone who is constantly about to throw up.

'Christ, darling. I think I am about to die.'

I offer some pancakes her way. She looks at them and retches. She runs to the bathroom and I can hear the sound of vomiting. I only hope she made it in time.

Scarlet is the next one to come down the stairs. She does not look hungover. She looks serene. Then I remember; Scarlet never drinks. Ever. The mix of losing control and toxins going into her body is a big no no for her.

'Did you have fun last night?' I ask her.

'Oh, yes, I did indeed darling. What a triumph for you. You did so well. That should get you at least one job.'

I try to ignore the seed of negativity she has planted in my mind, but I know it will blossom later.

'We made most of the papers.' I aim this at William but Scarlet assumes I am talking to her. She comes over and rifles through them. Her gestures seem more and more exaggerated the more papers she looks at.

'I'm not in any of them.' She is angry and indignant. After every paper is roughly skipped through, they end up crumpled, some of them are even on the floor. I think about what my reaction should be. I always think about what my reaction should be before I react. It is my greatest asset.

'Scarlet, please pick up the papers and sort them.'

She looks at me, burning with anger. I cannot understand how she is not censoring herself and at least trying to be gracious and polite. My anger stays where it is supposed to; under a veneer of politeness. It is not always wise to let people know how you feel.

Scarlet starts to smile, a thin, cruel smile. 'Of course, your highness.'

I sigh and roll my eyes. The masking is over. Why does she have to always be such a rude bitch. She picks the papers off the floor but does not fix them.

Scarlet goes into the fridge and takes out a natural yoghurt and some strawberries. She mixes the two and eats.

'Can I get you some coffee, Scarlet?' William asks, taking the papers, smoothing them down and sorting them together. William is the ultimate peacekeeper. He has learnt a lot from being a parent

'No thanks, I don't drink caffeine. A water would be good, though.'

William gets her some filtered water. She looks up and gives him a look of disdain.

'Do you not have any bottled water? Evian?'

'Of course.'

William goes to the fridge, takes out a bottle and gives it to her. Scarlet gives him a look as if he was trying to cheat her with the filtered water. She follows this with a sarcastic, 'Thanks.'

'I'm just going to check on Claudia. She's been a while.'

'Oh, yeah, I heard her puking. She always was a lightweight.'

'That from someone who doesn't even drink,' I say to Scarlet, giving her a glare.

'I drink.'

'Of course, you do.'

Scarlet is one of those people who will never admit the amount of work it takes to stay fit and healthy. She watches what she eats but will always say she eats what she wants. She claims her favourite meal is a burger and chips, and it probably is, but she usually eats healthy plant-based meals. She has regular work done but preaches in interviews about how she would never do that and how natural beauty is the most important thing. She pretends to be an earth mother but her clothes cost either hundreds or thousands. She has a veneer of hippy fake covering a corporate fame-hungry operator.

I walk to the bathroom. Claudia is slumped forwards onto the loo, head on hands. She looks like she is staying down for dear life.

'Are you okay?'

'Yes, just a little fragile. Do not worry about me.'

I squat down beside her and stroke her hair. Other than my husband and my children, Claudia is my only true friend in life. We have fallen out, sure, but our love has always brought us back together. I kiss the top of her head.

'I will go and get you some water. And a cushion for your knees. We're not getting any younger.'

Claudia manages a laugh. I get a bottle of Evian and a cushion and take it to her.

'Take a moment and let me know if you need anything else.'

Claudia says a "thank you" that sounds more like a whimper. I close the door to give her some privacy.

When I go back into the kitchen Scarlet is on the phone to Alex. She bitches about him all the time to me but now she is being all lovey-dovey. It is all "honey" and "sweetie". She rings off by telling him she loves him.

'How is Bear?' I ask her.

'Oh, he's fab. He's at a Montessori weekend. It's all the rage.'

I stifle a laugh. All the mothers at the children's nurseries were obsessed with Montessori. It is so achingly affected.

'Oh my God, I keep meaning to ask Tash, have you seen this?' Scarlet asks as she hands me her phone.

'Seen what?' I take the phone. It is an article in the leading entertainment magazine about me. It is titled 'Is Natasha Jones Over?' The cover image of me makes me look old and way too thin. It is the most unflattering angle I have ever seen. I begin to read.

*Natasha Jones is the Scottish actress who dropped her accent and went to RADA. Her early career was full of lucky breaks but she has yet to reach her potential, despite the fact she is forty-years-old. Forty is a scary age for any actress, but for one who trades on her looks like Natasha Jones does, it is even more so.*

*Jones has starred in a number of romantic comedies and even some action movies but none have had much artistic merit. Now it is time to see that she is too blonde, too thin and too bland to survive in the industry any more. She may be a well-connected fashion horse but we want our actors to have more depth now. In this article we do a post-mortem of her career and ask; whatever happened to Natasha Jones?*

Below this is a breakdown of every film I have ever done with a vicious critique. Wow! This journalist hates me. Truly.

'What's wrong, Mummy?' It is Amelia.

'Mum, are you okay?' Joseph is concerned too. The children hate it when I am sad. They will do anything they can to cheer me up. They may wind me up sometimes but they are the most wonderful, caring and loving people.

William walks past the kitchen island and puts his arm around me. I look into his eyes. They are full of concern. He takes the phone from me and has a look. Then he puts it down on the island.

I look at Scarlet who has a look of absolute glee on her face. She wants to see me breakdown. She wants tears. I will not give them to her.

'Thank you for sharing that with me, Scarlet. There is no such thing as bad feedback.' I give her my biggest smile. 'Right, it's my birthday weekend. We need tea and cake.'

This has the children cheering. William goes to make a pot and get the cake. I will be damned if I let that bitch ruin my weekend.

'God, guys, please keep it down. Someone is dying in here.'

We all laugh, apart from Scarlet. I just want her to leave. She is no longer my friend. She will never hurt me again.

# Chapter 25

## Then

I have my headphones on and I'm reading a book. Yet it is hard to concentrate when you keep catching a glimpse of a woman who is getting painted from head to toe while naked, well apart from a tiny red G string, but that is not covering much. She should have used some dental floss. It would have been kinder to my eyes.

The nude lady is nonchalantly browsing her phone. Which is better than when she first came in and admired herself in the mirror for ages after she took off her robe. The film I am doing is low budget, joy of joys. It means the food will be terrible and everyone will resent being here. The make-up is one big room where the production company also work. The costume 'department' is in a room off to the side. Ah, the glamour. I can barely take it.

There is silence in the rest of the room as everyone tries to ignore the preening nude woman.

'How long have you been a make-up artist?' I ask the woman doing my make-up. She looks ill at ease, even though she must deal with naked people all the time.

'Ten years.'

'Wow! That's amazing. What a career!'

She smiles at me.

'Thank you. I love your films. You're an amazing actress. I was excited to see you on the call sheet.'

The compliment is too vague to be genuine but I smile and thank her anyway. Something is better than nothing, I guess.

Finally, nude lady's body paint is finished but she refuses the robe. I wonder how the men in the office are handling this. Or if they will mention this when their other half asks about their day. A woman from the production office goes over to nude lady.

'Do you mind putting your robe on now? This is a working office. It is making the women who work here uncomfortable. Thank you.'

Nude lady sheepishly puts on the robe. A level of normality resumes.

I look at myself in the mirror. Dark circles painted on, even paler skin, crap hair. The make under has been achieved.

I don't want to be on camera looking as hideous as this, but vanity is the death of good acting. The film industry wants the women in it to be as beautiful as possible but then it does not take them seriously. They have to break themselves down and atone for their beauty to be taken seriously. It is all so fucked up.

The costume I am wearing is gross and I have a fake pregnancy stomach on me. It is heavy and weird. The clothes are as old-looking and scratchy as the clothes of my youth. I am playing a junkie and there are track marks up and down my arms. It looks so gross. I take a deep breath. At least I am working. A job is a job.

'You are done,' the make-up artist says.

'Thanks.'

I go to the holding area and grab a cup of tea. I take out my book and listen to my iPod while I wait to be taken to set. I am just getting into my book when the AD comes to get me. His eyebrows raise as he sees me. It is Sam, we have worked together on loads of films.

'Hi, Sam.'

'Hey, Natasha. Great to see you again. I was excited when I saw you on the call sheet.'

'I'm excited to see you too, Sam. You are my favourite AD.

Sam blushes.

'Follow me. It's time to go to set.'

I am acting opposite Edward Robb today and I can barely contain my excitement. He is a powerhouse. The actors' actor. I feel a nervousness that is different from the other films I have acted in. I trained at RADA for God's sake and here I am, shivering in my boots. I have heard that he can be intimidating. That he can get a bit "method". I calm my breathing to settle myself. You can't fail on film sets. Every job is an audition for the next.

We walk to the set and I see him. He does look intense. Acting opposite Edward Robb will keep my skills sharp and is going to make me look like a serious actress. Which I am, of course.

Sam introduces me to Edward Robb. He is not a good-looking man. He has a face that is a cross between a bulldog and a boxer who has taken more punches than most. He is the same height as me and stocky. His eyes are blue, as most actors' eyes are, for some reason. Even mine. He has hair as black as a raven and he is wearing clothes as shit as mine. I saw him earlier arriving with his blonde, glamorous wife. She was heavily pregnant and surprisingly age-appropriate.

'Hey Ed, this is Natasha. She's a fantastic actress. She will be playing Linda today.'

Ed gives me an appreciative look up and down. It's a bit creepy.

'It's an honour to meet you, Mr Robb. I love your work.'

Well, that certainly stroked his ego. He looks like a puffed-up peacock. It is so easy to get men onside. A little bit of flattery and they are putty in your hands.

'Call me Ed, please,' he says as he takes my hand and kisses it. *Ew, what is this? The nineteenth century?* I keep a warm smile on my face. 'It does you good to not let people know how you feel about them.' A *grande dame* once told me. I took it to heart and it has helped my career immensely.

'Shall we go through the scene?' Sam asks us.

'No, I want to just do it. Rehearsal ruins the artist's process,' Ed says.

Sam looks at me with an impassive look on his face, but I can tell underneath he has been dealing with Ed's bullshit for the duration of this film. They have a weariness about them, ADs, it is probably why so many of them are coked up all the time.

'That's fine with me. I like to get straight into it.'

Ed laughs dirtily. Great. Now I have to watch what I say in case he takes it as an innuendo.

We go into the room where we are filming the scene. I am supposed to go into another room but as soon as the director yells action I realise I do not know which one. Fuck. What do I do now?

I just improvise and go into the room I feel my character would enter. Bad idea; nude lady and a nude lady friend are in there. Sandwiched in the middle is a young male actor who thinks all his dreams have come true at once. They were clearly supposed to go at it when the director called action because going, they are. Christ, this was a bad idea.

'And cut.'

I get out of that room as fast as I can, before it is seared into my brain forever.

'Well, she can't go in there!' I hear Ed loudly bitching to the director.

I walk out of the set, which is built like a house. The set design is impressive, it looks like the crack den it is supposed to be in the inside and on the outside it looks like a wooden shed and a basic one at that. It is amazing what they can do.

The director gives me a vacant look. 'You cannot go into that room. Stay in the one you are in. Ed will move.'

Good to know. If only we had blocked it out beforehand. We go again. I have to admit that acting opposite Ed is fantastic. He is as good as they say he is. Fearless even. The intensity of it is exhilarating. The scene ends.

'Cut!' the director says. I note the director is female. A rarity. She has streaks of blue and red through her hair and gold glasses on her face.

'That was great, really amazing. You're a good actor,' Ed says to me.

I blush and mumble a thank you. I wait for them to check the gate for hairs or other obstructions in the view of the camera. Ed wanders off again to talk to the director.

'Hey, Robyn, why don't we get my missus to come and act the part? She's pregnant. What do you think?'

I cannot believe what I am hearing. What a two-faced arsehole. He just told me I was a great actor and he loved what I was doing. Now he is trying to get me fired. And does he not realise that his voice is carrying? He is not exactly whispering.

I can hear the director trying to placate him.

'Most of the shot is already in the bag. We don't have the time and the money to start again,' Robyn tells him.

'Oh, come on, she would be great. She would be a great actor.'

'Let's just see how it goes.'

This is bullshit as this is my first scene. It would take them moments to replace me. Robyn is just too scared to tell him she does not want to. I am even ignoring the fact that I am in my twenties and his wife looks like she is in her forties. If she was not pregnant, I would go higher. I can hear him coming back. I feel crestfallen but I put a smile on my face. I do not want him to think that I heard.

I see a moment of guilt in his expression as our eyes meet. He gives me a smile. I stand up and go to my mark.

'Action!'

Then we go again. Funnily enough the scene is more intense this time. I will show this bastard. I will show all the bastards.

'And cut! We got it. That was perfect.'

Perfect. The scene is done. They will check the gate, of course, but I dare to hope. I wait.

'Yes, yes, that is great. Let's move onto the next scene.'

'Bye, Ed. Great working with you. Bye, Robyn, thank you so much for having me. Great script.'

That is my only scene today. I head to costume to get this fucking costume off. I walk there as fast as I can. I see the actor's wife doing make-up as I am about to open the door to costume. Unbelievable. She is a make-up artist! Not even an actress. He clearly already got her a job on this film, and still he is trying to move her up the next rung of the ladder. Next thing you know he will be suggesting she directs. What a joke. I grab my clothes. I take off my costume and the fake stomach. The weight leaving my body feels amazing. I put on my own clothes and leave as quickly as possible. I need to take the tube home. The film is so low budget there is no transport. Ed got a driver, of course. I had seen that twat in so many films and admired him. Never again. He had worked with Spielberg and Scorsese. He is a British institution and, it turns out, a complete jerk. I wonder if that is what it takes to make it. No morals and no spine. I would rather do something else with my life if so.

The tube takes ages to arrive which does not improve my mood. There are also no free seats so I can't even read my book. I watch the world as it goes by and there is plenty to see on a trip from east London to west. When I finally arrive home, I feel as if I have travelled the entire country. Only then, do I remember the make-up I am wearing, and that I still have track marks all over my arms. I forgot to wipe them off. Ah, good old London. No one even batted an eyelid.

*Now*

What goes up must come down. The article started a backlash. I went from darling British actress done good to a jumped up, anorexic, over-privileged, talentless bitch. Completely untrue articles about my diva behaviour ended up in the trashy celebrity mags. *Popbitch* had a few of me that were true but from a bad day here and there. Everyone has bad days or days when they are grumpy. But when you are famous, they become who you are. That person only meets you when you are in a bad mood and they tell everyone they ever met that you are a bitch. The tabloids publish the nude pictures from my first ever film. It is a pile on.

Paparazzi are outside of our home every day. I feel that I am suffocating but it is nothing compared to the pain of seeing my family going through all this shit. The children get bullied at school and harassed by the paparazzi. They save the worst of their viciousness for William and I. They wave nude pictures in William's face and ask what it is like to be married to such a bitch of a wife. The onslaught is shocking. You would think I murdered someone. I start to hate my country and the tall poppy syndrome within it. British people hate successful people. They hate rich people more than anything.

We keep thinking, it will die down but it doesn't, and I know that my London dream is now over. We need to escape.

I take hundreds of auditions. Literally. Self-tape after self-tape, meeting after meeting. I cannot find a job. Instead of panic, a calmness comes over me. I had a good run. Maybe, now is a good time to go and do other things. I walk through our huge house and I wonder why we need it. I look at all my designer clothes and all of the clutter. I look for the truth in the backlash. All the negative comments need some good to come from them. The truth is I have chased role after role with no plan. I just wanted to act. As long as a role was respectful to women, I took it. I should have worked harder on my artistic integrity. My life has filled up on the superficial.

Everything feels like it is suffocating me. I need to be free of everything. The bones of me are William, Joseph and Amelia. I do not need anything else. All of this has to go.

We put the house on the market. We get a buyer quickly but have nowhere else to go. Thankfully, the buyer is patient while we decide what to do next. I should have been more organised instead of starting everything on a whim.

It takes a huge amount of planning but the next step finally comes. We will move to New York. Away from the paparazzi, away from the bullying children. New Yorkers will not care about me. I will be able to walk around without bother. The paparazzi will stay in London. I hope so, anyway. The main motivation for the move comes because I am sick of running away from what scares me the most. I am going to do theatre. Broadway, here I come.

*Then*

It takes years for the film I did with Nadia Sharma to come out. This is not unusual, but it is frustrating. You can wait for years. Some do not come out at all. I go with Claudia, her latest boyfriend, some banker called Geoff and William. I can hardly contain my excitement.

We go the whole hog; popcorn, cola, nachos, chocolate and pic 'n' mix. We all sit in the darkened theatre and wait. I recognise the scene when it starts and my heart leaps. I am on the edge of my seat, but then it finishes. I have been cut out. My scene is gone. I am devastated but I try and hide it. I whisper to William that I am going to the bathroom and I leave the theatre. I call Louise.

She answers on the first ring.

'Hi, Natasha.'

'Hi, Louise, I just went to the cinema to see Right Here Now and I wasn't in it.'

'Oh, dear, sorry, darling. I should have told you. Apparently, you pissed off Suzanne Thorogood. Why would you do that, darling? That was very silly indeed. She's a powerhouse in the industry. Everyone bows to her.'

I feel rage surge through me. Suzanne is always doing interviews about empowering women. She describes herself as a feminist and yet, every man, I have worked with, says she is supportive and got them work, and every woman is terrified of her and says she hates younger women. This is why men run the industry, not only because of their inherent male entitlement, but also because women see each other as the enemy. We are pitted against each other and buy into the whole women-hate-other-women thing.

'Thank you for letting me know, Louise.' I hang up. There is no more to say. I take a moment to gather myself.

I go back into the cinema and sit in-between Claudia and William. Claudia pats my knee. She knows. Her intuition is always great. William has not clocked that I have been cut out yet. I don't want to tell him. We watch the rest of the film together and I simmer. I will never forgive Suzanne for this. One day I will be a powerful, successful actress and then I will show her how it is really done.

# Chapter 26

## Now

I watch New York go by as I sip my coffee. They may be a cliché, but I love the yellow cabs. Everything is loud and brash. The people seem to walk faster and even talk faster. Everyone is in a rush. There is every type of person you could think of. It is impossible to visit New York and not feel like you have been here before. It is the most exciting sensory overload. The coffee tastes real here. I do not think I could go back to British coffee. My in-laws are coming today and so are my family. I have never been more excited to have my family around.

New York is a busy, bustling city but I have found a quietness here. I have put a brake on the relentless pursuit of fame and fortune. I want to head for success instead. The past six months has made me miss my anonymity. It was the price I paid before and that price turned out to be too high.

I finish my coffee and I go to get dressed. Blue jeans, not even designer, they are from Uniqlo. As is my aqua blue T-shirt and black cardigan. I put on some old-school Adidas sneakers and take a last look in the mirror before I head out. Not too much make up; only mascara, lip balm and concealer. Hair done up in a messy top knot. I put my max mara coat on and grab my navy blue satchel.

I am a little heavier. A healthy size ten. It was not even a conscious decision. I just started eating burgers again. I used to eat my emotions all the time. I do not want to go back there but I want to treat myself sometimes. It turns out gluten, diary and sugar were not the enemy after all.

We lease the brownstone we are renting for a bargain price from a hedge fund friend of William's. It really pays off to have rich friends. We have an open invitation to join him on his yacht for a holiday. My life is quieter, but just as luxurious.

I walk to a local café I love. I am meeting Patricia Anderson there. She is an actress, or actor I should say, apparently the word 'actress' is sexist now – I say, pick your battles – who's work I have admired my entire life. She is from an acting dynasty, born and raised in LA with a string of failed marriages behind her. She is almost fifty and a size fourteen. Both crimes for a woman in the acting industry. Patricia is gorgeous. From head to toe. Small standards of beauty only belong to the women's magazines who use them to make women feel like shit about themselves, because the lower your self-esteem the more money they can get you to spend.

The owner gives me a barely perceptible smile and a nod as soon as I walk in. I give one back. No one notices me, or ignores me if they do. I can see Patricia at the back. She has a pot of tea and a Danish pastry. Patricia knows how to live. I am sick of beige actresses who are afraid of real food and living a real life. The actress I used to be. I wasn't even living a life. I was a Barbie.

'Hey.'

'Hey, Patricia.'

Patricia stands up and gives me a warm hug. I hug her back.

'I got a pot of tea and two cups. I wasn't sure if you took sugar or milk so I got both.'

'That is great, thank you. I love tea. It runs the world, right?'

'Too true. You're British, right?'

'Yes, I am.' I think about saying Scottish-British but it complicates things so I leave it.

'Thank you for meeting me. I love the work you're doing.'

'Thank you, Patricia. That means so much to me.' I almost well up at her compliment.

We both sit down. There is a warmth at this table. Mutual respect and sisterhood.

'I'm so happy you took this meeting. I have such a girl crush on you, you are so talented and I love the films you make. We need more of you. This industry is rotten from the inside out. We need to be the change we want.'

Patricia clasps her hands to her chest in a moment of absolute glee.

'That's amazing, Natasha. I cannot tell you how much this means to me. We do need to change this industry and we can.' Patricia takes my hand after she says this. We stay there for a moment, taking it in. Full of hope.

'I brought some scripts,' I say as I take them out of my satchel. 'I have bought options to some good books. I wrote the scripts myself, so be kind. We can always hire someone else, or work on them together.'

Patricia takes them. She goes into her bag and takes out a notepad and a pen.

'Do not doubt yourself, Natasha. They doubt us all the time. Be brave and put yourself out there knowing you are just as good as everyone else.'

I take her words, imprint them on my mind, my heart.

'Thank you.'

We have another moment of looking at each other. I know now that Patricia is one of the team. We are going to do amazing things.

'This one is my favourite. It is about three women who start out as enemies and then become friends. They start to work together to overcome the forces against them. I know, I know, metaphors ahoy, but it is the script of Away Day, that book that was on the bestseller list for months.'

'I read that. It was brilliant. Let me see the script.'

I hand it over to Patricia and she puts on her glasses and starts reading. I am reminded of her acceptance speech for the Oscar she won a few years ago. She committed the crime of being political during her acceptance speech and Hollywood decided to punish her, as it tends to do. Sometimes it lets you back in, after you have paid for your crime. Other actors, no matter how famous they have been in the past or how much money they have made for the studio, are cast out forever. Has-beens relegated to the 'where are they now?' column of newspapers and magazines. Journalists never forget though; they hunt down the has-beens and pick over their bones. Once you have been famous you can never go back.

I put the other four scripts out on the table, along with my pen and Moleskine notebook. The nerves are right in my throat, tightening it. I have to put my hands on the table to stop them shaking.

I pour a mug of tea and I add milk and a cube of sugar. So unlike me but I think the sugar will help my blood-sugar and I have always preferred tea with milk. Patricia nudges the plate of Danish pastries to me. I take one. I have Soul Cycle later. I have not let go of wanting to stay in shape, even if I am more relaxed about it.

Patricia is a fast reader. I know she reads a lot of books. Her Instagram account is full of a book club she started. She may be in Hollywood purgatory, doing a TV show on a tiny cable channel. The TV show is great and has a huge following, but adoration from fans and critical acclaim are different. The film industry is full of rules. Rules that need to be broken.

I sip my tea and eat the pastry and people watch. It is my favourite thing. Being able to do so is a privilege. You cannot watch people when they are watching you.

After what feels like an age, Patricia looks up.

'Natasha, I think this is brilliant. I want to do it. You are such a good writer.'

I want to scream but I hold it in. Patricia is the first person I have shown my writing to. I have spent my life putting my actual self out there but showing my writing to people always took more courage than I had at that moment.

'Wow! That's everything. I am so happy. Welcome to Phoenix productions. We are going to do amazing things together.'

'Yes, we are. Are you going to direct it?'

'I would like to direct again, but I was thinking of Nadia Sharma.'

Patricia's face lights up. 'I love Nadia Sharma. She mixes Bollywood and Hollywood together seamlessly.'

'Yes, she really does.'

'Let me see the other scripts.'

I hand them over.

'They are all female-centric. We are not against men of course, they can have good roles too, but we need to readjust the balance. No one will be forced to do nude scenes either. It will be an amazing, safe space to work in.'

Patricia looks at me and smiles. She takes my hand again.

'What you're doing is amazing, Natasha. It's been a long time coming. Thank you from me and everyone else. We are going to do so much good.'

I squeeze her hand back.

'Yes, yes we are.'

*Then*

The sound of my phone wakes me up. At least I think it is my phone. I check the baby monitor. All safe on the kiddie front. I had tried to stay up late for the Oscar nominations, like I do every year. I do not have a hope in hell of being nominated, despite what the many journalists who have interviewed me say.

I got a role in an amazing indie movie after the Suzanne Thorogood table fiasco. Turns out the puppet mistress does not control every string. It was a lead role and it sparked the imagination of the press who decided it was the movie of the year. Critical acclaim followed. It feels good after all my shitty luck.

I open my eyes. Fuck, I have spilt some wine on the sofa. Thankfully, it is white wine. William is snoring next to me. It is sweet he wanted to stay up too. My phone starts to ring again and I answer it. I am still half asleep.

'Hello.'

'Natasha, how do you feel?'

'What?'

'How do you feel? This is amazing. What an achievement!'

*What the actual fuck is Louise on about!*

'Natasha, could you possibly not know?'

'Know what?' My eyelashes feel as if they are glued together. I have to peel my eyes open.

'You have been nominated for an Oscar.'

It feels like the world is slowing down. I cannot believe what I am hearing and yet I know the words are true. I try to nudge William awake but he is sound asleep. He once slept through a fire alarm at a hotel we were staying at. It took actual violence to wake him up.

I place my hand on the sofa to steady myself. I am too scared to believe the truth. If I take this in, then I might lose it. That is what happens when happy things happen, right? They get swept out from under you.

'Are you there?'

I breathe in and out. Calm myself. Centre myself. It's working. I take a finger and prod William in the side. Hard. He wakes.

'What is it?'

I look at him and I can't say anything. I'm in shock.

'Natasha?' Louise is still trying to get something out of me.

'Thank you, Louise. Thank you for telling me. That's excellent news.'

'The world is your oyster now, Natasha. Your career has moved on to a whole other level. Try to get some sleep. Speak soon.' Louise hangs up.

William is still looking at me.

'It's the Oscars, isn't it? You won, didn't you?'

The air comes back to me. Slowly.

'Nominated. I was nominated.'

'Yes!' William jumps up, his fists wave triumphantly. I watch his joy and take it in. I still feel like I am in shock. The numbness is still there.

'You know what this calls for, my darling?'

William takes my face in his hands and gives me a deep, passionate kiss on the lips. I look up at him, his beauty. He is a stunning man. He has the most unique, gorgeous green eyes I have ever seen. His jaw is perfect and his cheekbones would make any woman jealous. His brown hair has become lighter after our holiday in Italy. He is tanned, tall and toned. He is beautiful enough to be a movie star himself but, instead, he chose to be a human rights lawyer. Looks, heart, brains. Wham bam, the entire trifecta. Finally, I find my voice amongst all my good fortune.

'What does it call for, my love?'

'Champagne.'

William and I always keep a good bottle of champagne in case a moment ever calls for it. The moments tend to call for it a lot. Sometimes the reason for the celebration is the mere fact we have a bottle of champagne in the fridge. I smile at him.

'Sounds wonderful.'

He goes to the kitchen cabinet to get the glasses and the wine. He comes back with two glasses in the expensive Waterford coupes that were a wedding present from Brenda, my mother-in-law. They are gorgeous. He gives me the green one because he knows it is my favourite colour. We toast.

'To Natasha Jones, world famous, Oscar-nominated actress.' William gives me a wink and then we both take a drink. I pinch myself. I actually pinch myself. No matter how much it feels as if I have stepped into a different realm, it is all still real.

We stay up for the rest of the night. The excitement is too much to sleep. We fuck twice and then eat what is in the fridge. His Girl Friday with Rosalind Russell is on the television and we get excited. It is one of our favourite films.

When dawn breaks the messages come flooding in. Scarlet sends me, *well done xx*. Claudia sends: *I knew it. I*

*felt it in my bones. You are a superstar. So well deserved*
*darling xxx.*

It makes me happy inside. Brenda, my siblings, even
my parents send a message. My publicist calls at ten. She
has been fielding calls and emails all day. It starts to hit me
and then it sits there, the truth of it all; I have finally made
it. I am untouchable now. There is only up from here.

# Chapter 27

## Now

Autumn. A time for renewal. Autumn has always been my favourite season. Summer has too many insects and sticky sunscreen. When your skin is as pale as mine the sun is not your friend. Can a summer's day really rival the beauty of autumn leaves? I think not. Winter in New York will be brutal, I know that, but brutal is character building. It will be good for the children. I love snow. The sound it makes underneath your shoes, the joy of a cup of cocoa while the world is covered in a dazzling blanket of white. It is just glorious.

'You look out of the window a lot. Has anyone ever told you that? Amelia does it too – takes after her mother.'

'I guess I do, Brenda. I'm a bit of a daydreamer.'

'And all the better for it. Look where it got you. A tough working-class Scot becomes an Oscar-winning movie star. No mean feat.'

I wish I could make Brenda my inner voice. I would never doubt myself ever again.

'Thank you, Brenda, you are always so kind and thank you for coming. I know it's a long way.'

'No love, thank you for sending us the ticket. First class too. You didn't have to do that. You're always so generous.'

Brenda makes me feel warm inside. Most of the other people I do things for are not grateful. They just expect it, like my success is their success. My money, their money. It makes me angry.

I rush towards Brenda and I give her a huge hug. I breathe her in and squeeze her. She is taken aback but she takes it in her stride. My mother walks in mid-hug. She does not look happy. My mother and I have never been close, but we have both worked hard at our relationship in recent years. We try to avoid the things that trigger each of us. It is not an easy relationship, but somehow, we make it work.

'Hello, Mary. How was the flight?' Brenda asks my mother in a guarded way. She knows she bites.

'It was a bit extravagant. Other than that, it was pleasant. Bit long though.'

I roll my eyes. If I had not sent her first class, she would have made comments about how 'cheap' her rich daughter was. Christ. There is no pleasing some people.

'Anyway, I think everything is ready. William has been slaving away as usual. You really should be more domestic, Natasha. It's not really fair on him. It's probably why he cheated on you. Men like to be taken care of.'

'Mum, honestly, do not be such a dinosaur and William did not cheat on me. That woman kissed him when he was drunk. If anything, it was sexual assault.

241

Imagine if the genders were reversed. There would have been an outcry. It would have been a Me Too moment.'

'Oh, Natasha, all of this Me Too stuff. It's so silly. Men are scared to even look at a woman now. It's such a shame. I mean, you're lucky because you are married, but imagine how hard it is for your sister. Men are too scared to say boo to a goose.'

Brenda squeezes my arm. My mother notices and her eyes narrow. I go for the easy path. If I placate her ego, all will be okay and she will calm down. Her behaviour will go from obliteration to merely bitchy.

'Oh, Mum, let's stop being silly. Is supper ready? Let's go through. I'm hungry. You must be starving.'

'It's dinner, Natasha. How can you lose your Scottish roots so easily? Supper is the meal in-between dinner and bedtime.'

The tiger does not want to go back in its cage.

'There is a meal in-between dinner and bedtime?' Brenda looks genuinely confused. 'Well, maybe you should give that up, Mary. You don't want to get tubby.'

With that Brenda walks past my mother who has her mouth hanging open. I use my training not to laugh. The respect I have for Brenda is enormous. It takes a lot to be brave enough to stand up to bullies.

'Come on, Mum, it will get cold.'

My mother follows me through. She is fuming. Her face has gone a deep crimson shade and her lips have stretched thin. It is not a good look.

'Let's all just get along and have fun. This is New York. You always wanted to come here.'

My mother just gives me a look and heads to the other side of the table. Oh well. I tried.

I love this kitchen. It's modern and stainless steel. The dining table is huge and could feed fifty people. Everything in the kitchen hides away so it never looks cluttered.

I go to the head of the table near William. He gives me a kiss on the lips. Happiness surges through me. I sit down in my seat. The food looks amazing. William has cooked a chicken roast but it is more like a Christmas dinner. There are pigs in blankets, parsley sauce, cranberry sauce, roast vegetables, a huge chicken roasted in honey and herbs. My mouth is watering just looking at it. For pudding William baked chocolate muffins, a Victoria sponge and a chocolate cake. One could certainly get fat on all of this and it would be worth it.

The children do their bit by pouring champagne into everyone's glass.

'It's all a bit much, don't you think?' I hear my mother fake whisper to my dad. He nods his head in agreement. When everyone has champagne, the children sit down. William clinks his glass.

'If I could have your attention, please.'

Everyone looks at William.

'We have some news. As you all know, Natasha has her Broadway debut tomorrow and you are all invited to that, but that is not the only exciting thing that is happening. And, no, I'm not talking about the marvellous films she is making either.' William pauses for effect. He has picked up a few things along the way. A few eyebrows are raised, I can tell no one has any idea.

'Natasha is pregnant.'

My mother spits out her champagne. Serves her right, drinking it before the toast.

'But she's so old.' This comes from my sister.

'Thanks Stephanie. That's a nice thing to say.'

Everyone looks surprised, apart from the children who already knew. No one says anything. It is uncomfortable.

'She's right, Natasha. You are quite old.' My mother gestures at the other children. 'Think of the age gap. And when you get to your age there are so many complications.'

William looks pissed off beyond measure.

'Well, I say the more the merrier. Well done, you two. How exciting, another grandchild!' Brenda saves the day again. I feel sad that her heart does not seem to be in it.

'A toast. Our family are so happy to have another addition coming soon. Life couldn't be better.'

Everybody raises their glass and then drinks but the mood is all off. The evening is ruined.

'Well, I'm excited to have another sibling,' Amelia says. She screamed for five full minutes when we told her. She loves babies.

'So am I. I hope I get a brother,' Joseph loudly states.

Amelia elbows Joseph.

'No offence, sis.'

Amelia playfully rolls her eyes at him. They are such a team. My biggest success in life is how my children have turned out, and how much they love each other. I look at

William, who is putting a brave face on. He has made such an effort and people are so ungrateful. It reminds me that I need to keep my world small. I have to be careful about who I let in.

# Chapter 28

## Then

I get a call about the delivery. It's top secret and I'm not to let anyone know. A courier will arrive on a motorbike. Considering the value of the item, I understand why precautions are being taken. I am nervous as hell.

Twenty minutes later there is a knock on the door. The courier still has his helmet on, I can't see his face. He hands me the bags and heads off.

I place the bags down and smooth them. I am almost too scared to open them. Inside is a dream. I unzip the first one. It is red and delicate. Givenchy says the label. I gasp. I take it out and hang it up. I can barely believe that I have been sent this. It is bigger than my biggest dream.

I open the next one; *Oscar de la Renta.* A pale-blue off-the-shoulder chiffon dress with ruffles. I have a fashiongasm when I see it. The others are from Versace and Gucci. All these people want to dress me. I have never felt so lucky in my life. Well, other than when I got the nomination. These clothes must be worth tens of thousands of pounds. I Facetime Claudia. I have to share this moment with someone who will understand.

'Hey, Oscar-nominated actress.'

'Hey, gorgeous actress.'

Claudia does her thinking face while stroking a pretend beard.

'I'll take it.'

'Look at these.' I turn the camera around and show her the showroom my living room has become. She screams.

'Oh my fucking God! I am coming over. Right now.'

I laugh. I figured as much.

'See you soon.'

I hang up and go into the kitchen. I take out some wine and two glasses. I put some olives and crisps into a bowl. I may as well make an event of it. I scroll Twitter and Instagram while I wait for her. The knock on the door comes quickly.

Claudia is breathless when I open the door.

'Fuck's sake. I am so unfit.'

I give her a kiss on the cheek. She goes straight into the kitchen for some water. She downs the glass in a minute. Then she sees the wine and pours. She puts my glass on the coffee table and then sits on the sofa.

'Right, now is the movie montage time. One after the other. Then I might try one on.' She makes a coy innocent look.

I try the first one on. It is tight on the hips and stomach. I look like a sausage stuffed into a too-tight casing.

'Oh darling, maybe you should send it back for a bigger size.'

'They do not do bigger sizes. You either fit into sample size or you don't. For most designers, anyway.

Claudia pulls a face. 'Well, that is bloody stupid. Clothes should be made to fit women, women's bodies should not be altered to fit the dress. You can tell most designers are men. They never design for boobs either. It is so bloody annoying. Maybe we should start our own line.'

'I get your point but I cannot keep raging against the machine. Maybe when I have more power, but never mind. I have time to lose the weight. The camera adds ten pounds after all. I've been celebrating far too much. I have become an expert at getting into shape quickly. The most important thing to remember is that you cannot out-exercise a bad diet. The biggest thing is not to starve yourself because then you fuck up your metabolism.'

Despite her feminist protestations, I can tell she is interested.

'I am listening.'

'You need to cut out sugar and junk food.'

Claudia rolls her eyes. 'All of the good stuff and live on rabbit food.'

'No, there are plenty of good foods you can eat, but nothing comes easy in life. Your health and a good body are things you need to work for. I know is it is unfair but staying in shape is part of your job as an actress. You also have to stay fit for those long fourteen-hour days.

'You cut out the junk, record what you eat so you can see what your weakness is. Count calories, make your diet plant-based, start the day with a green smoothie. Exercise every day. HIIT some days, strength training others. Yoga is good for a warm up or a cool down because it calms the body.'

'Oh, is that all? Sounds easy.' The sarcasm is dripping from her. I love it when Claudia is sarcastic.

'We could do it together. Be gym buddies.'

'You know, I would love that. Wait, don't you have a personal trainer and a dietician?'

I laugh, she got me.

'Yes, I do, and I am willing to share both. After all, you are coming with me, right?'

'To where?'

'The Oscars.'

Her first reaction is shock but then she screams and jumps up. She almost knocks me over with the force of her hug. I hug her back.

'I cannot imagine not having my best friend there on such a special day.'

'You mean your other best friend.'

I look at her and blink.

'William. You think I don't know that he has replaced me?'

'Oh, darling, he did not replace you, he only complemented the set.'

Claudia does a pretend cry.

'Good. I will share if I have to but he cannot have you all to himself.'

'Go and try on one of the dresses.'

Claudia kisses me full on the lips.

'You are the best friend ever. I love you.'

She tries on the *Oscar de la Renta*. It fits perfectly and looks stunning on her.

'You bitch.'

She nods nonchalantly. 'Yeah, yeah, I know.'

*Now*

William and I lie in bed after the supper fiasco. I love our bedroom. It has a huge bed in it. It is probably double the size of a normal king size. There is only the bed, two bedside tables and some plants in this room. It has a walk-in wardrobe to the left. It has both shutters and thick, heavy, grey curtains which block out both noise and light.

The pared back decluttered thing helps me relax. I come in here when I need to think.

It was a long night. I keep trying to be an easy-going, family-oriented person but I feel bruised by the experience. I do not know if it is me, or them.

'It's not your fault. You did your best.'

It is as if he can read my mind. He can, of course. We have been together for so long he knows me up and down, inside and out.

'Brenda did not seem that happy about the baby. I was surprised by that.'

'It's just because we live in New York now. She knows she's going to miss out on most of it. With the other two she was always there. She helped us raise them.'

I face palm myself. Of course. How could I not have realised?

'When do you think we will announce it?'

I look at William, confused. 'We just did.'

'I mean to the press.'

My body does a mini-reel inside. I might vomit. I will never announce anything about my personal life to the press ever again. They are vipers, waiting to turn on a dime. I will never make that pact with Satan ever again.

'We are not.'

'What do you mean?'

'What do you mean, "What do I mean"? I am never going back into that fucked up pact, William. They completely destroyed me.'

William rolls his eyes.

'It wasn't that bad, darling. Just think about it. The public deserve to know. You are twelve weeks now.'

He heads to the bathroom. The "public" Who the hell is this man and what did he do with my husband? People change in the years you are married to them. Sometimes for the better and sometimes for the worst. But they will never stop surprising you.

William comes out, toothbrush in his mouth. I sit up.

'William, I'm an actor. Nothing more, nothing less. I'm just a person with a job. I'm not the bloody Prime Minister. My private life is my own. I'm no longer offering up parts of myself.'

William blinks.

'Oh, Natasha, be realistic.'

'About what?'

'The press is never going to lose their interest. Unless you move to a ranch then you have to give a bit.'

'Yes, William, with my work, but not my personal life. I owe no one anything about my personal life. I cannot believe you want to offer our unborn child up as a news story.'

This hits the mark. He goes back into the bathroom to spit.

'Tash, I know you are upset and you have had a rough ride, but the optics of a new baby works so well. What better way to gain redemption?'

'You make it sound like I murdered someone, William. I made the mistake of being rich, blonde and thin. It is hardly OJ Simpson territory.'

'We lost touch of the PR narrative. People like down to earth people. We forgot that.'

I have never heard William talk like this before and I do not like it.

'People hate successful people. They hate the rich, the beautiful and the thin. Some people, maybe even most people, but who cares? Should we all not work and let ourselves go? Should we constantly make ourselves smaller for other people? So we don't upset their egos or make them feel bad about themselves. People hate anything they perceive to be unearned. They hate lucky people and happy people. The tabloids are the worst of this. The knife edge of the worst of humanity; bitterness and jealousy. We all have it deep down but the press whip it up. *Schadenfreude,* William. There is always some terrible person getting pleasure from someone else's suffering because it makes them feel better about their shit lives.'

William moves his head to the side and I can see him think.

'Great rant, darling. Lots of truth.'

I roll my eyes. I do that a lot lately.

'I was punished for being a middle-aged woman. That was my crime; being female and ageing. No, scrub that, just being female. I am never getting back in bed with the press. I would have to be stupid.'

William comes over and starts stroking my hair. He sits down beside me and cuddles into me.

'Well think about it, Tash. I know you're probably feeling overwhelmed right now and you want to protect our little bump, but a baby always warms people's hearts. You getting pregnant at forty is also great optics; it means you are still youthful and fertile.'

There are so many things to argue about right now but I do not have the energy. I just crawl into bed and put the covers over myself. I do not wash my face or brush my teeth. My beauty routine is usually a twelve-step thing with multiple moisturisers, serums, oils and cleansers. I always floss – every single day. The constant work of womanhood. But not tonight. I close my eyes and hope for sleep.

'I was thinking, Tash, we have enough money and the new baby is coming. We will have a nanny and other staff to oversee. I think I should quit my job. I've been a lawyer for so long. It is starting to feel old and tedious. I helped a lot of people and I made money doing it. I could get a good golden handcuffs package. What do you think, Tash?'

I pretend I am asleep.

# Chapter 29

## Now

I step into my dressing room. There are flowers on almost every surface. Roses mostly, in many colours, tulips, lilies, and some more that I cannot remember the names of. It is a good thing I don't have hay fever. I look at the cards, there is one from Annabel, the editor of Stylish. I feel pride surge through me. I have still got it.

There are flowers from William and the children, Claudia and her family, many actors I have worked with, Alex and, separately, Scarlet. I read the one from Alex.

*Break a leg, Natasha! Alex.*

Careful, impersonal.

From Claudia and family, *Break a leg, superstar! Another huge achievement. So proud of you. Looking forward to seeing the show. Xx*

From my family,
*To our Mummy, you are the best, we are so proud of you.*
*Well done, my gorgeous wife. Break a leg. Xx*

I leave Scarlet until last. I have never forgiven her. I never will. Forgiveness is for pussies.

*To my oldest and dearest friend,*
*Break a leg. I love you, darling. I will be there tonight. See*
*you after the show! Xxx*

I let out a sigh. No matter how many times you take out the trash it keeps on coming back. I will let security know to keep that bitch away.

I sit down in front of the mirror and take out some stuff from my bag to make the room more homely. Better late than never. I place pictures of the children on my mirror and one of William and I on our wedding day. We look young and happy. It is funny how much he can annoy me. Yet even when times are rough there is a gravitational pull that keeps us together. Sometimes the pull is not love; it is memory and history and, yes, the children. You spend so many years building up your life together it feels unfathomable to pull it all down.

The buzz of New York fuels me. Broadway. It is prestigious. I never thought I would be here. Theatre has never been my thing. I hate working in the evening because then I miss seeing the children. Most actors hate doing theatre. It does not pay as well and is not permanent in the way that film is. Well, other than the luvvies who go on about their craft all the time and think they are superior because they are "artists". They look down on film actors, but put one of them on a film set and it is ham all the way. Fuck 'em!

Not that most actors admit it, but doing the same thing night after night is boring. But I need artistic integrity and theatre and independent films are the only way to do it. The film industry is all one big game, like snakes and ladders but much more vicious. I am working hard on my comeback. I am playing their stupid game. I am doing the things that are the right thing. The done thing. I am behaving, toeing the line.

Tonight is curtains up. This could be a disaster. I could crash and burn again. Failure is always on the horizon but I am brave. If I let failure scare me, I would still be on a council estate in Scotland, working some crappy job. The real courage is having the courage to fulfil your potential.

'Natasha, five minutes.'

The time is now. Curtain's up.

Waiting in the wings is terrifying. It's a full house. I ignore the faces. I am terrified. I want to run away and do something else. Quit acting, never put myself out there again but I have to get into the zone. I breathe in and out. I am okay, I am centred.

Then I step onto the stage. I walk to the spotlight, to where the light is hottest.

I take the moment in. They can all wait. I have earned this. Then I speak.

'They say, every woman is looking for a husband, but I am just looking for a good, hard drink.'

People laugh. Everything is in motion. It will be all right now.

'That was stunning, Tash. You were so powerful and sexy. I loved it.' Claudia is her usual self. Full of support and love.

'She was magnificent, wasn't she?' William gives me that look that I love. The one where the love pours from his eyes and I can tell he does not want to be anywhere else.

'I liked it,' says my mother begrudgingly.

'Yeah, it was good,' Stephanie adds. My brother nods.

'Thank you, everyone. I'm glad we found a restaurant that could fit us all in.'

Everyone laughs. There are a lot of people at this table. My family, William's family, Claudia's family, some people from the theatre. All the people I love are here.

'I think I am going to go all-out. Everyone please join us. Starter, main, pudding. You can all have champagne, of course.'

William gestures to the waiter who is standing at the door. We have our own private room of course. Sometimes coming across as down to earth does not matter to William after all. I giggle to myself and he gives me an amused look. We end up having a feast and I try to not think about how much exercise I need to do to burn off all of this. Two hours of cycling will probably be needed. All gain if no pain.

I order a lemonade. I want something fizzy to celebrate. I look around at my family as we eat and drink. I savour the moment of everyone being in the same place.

I take William's hand and give it a squeeze. Just as I do the baby gives a huge kick. I guess the latest addition did not want to be left out. This moment is perfect.

# Chapter 30

## Then

The preparation for the red carpet started six months in advance. Dress fittings, exercise regime, diet, hair and make-up tests. Fake tan applications, the works. I am a nervous wreck in the limo. William and Claudia are on either side of me, holding my hand. I wonder if this feeling ever goes away. I feel like I am right where I belong, yet I want to run away and hide to an easier life.

When we arrive, there is a line of limousines. More than I can count. Famous person after famous person step out of them. William's jaw hits the floor. Even Claudia, so unfazed by practically everything in life, looks like she might implode at the sight of Meryl Streep, closely followed by Tom Hanks. I make a conscious note to keep my mouth shut and my game face on. I do not want to look like a fan. I am on this side of the fence.

Now it is my turn. William gets out first and opens the door. He puts his hand out and smiles at me. I take it and, knees together, get out of the car. The cameras flash as soon as I do. I smile and I move aside for Claudia. William takes her hand too, ever the gentleman.

William walks the first few steps with me then he asks for my bag. I give it to him and go forwards alone. I walk to the mark and I pose. People call my name and I look this way and that. Claudia and I practised posing for hours. We took pictures and critiqued each other endlessly.

I motion for William to join me and we have a few pictures taken, then I motion for Claudia to stand with me and she does too. After it is finished, we go in. The entire thing is surreal. William gives me back my bag. It is full of nuts and chocolate to sustain us through the four-hour ceremony. The Oscars are famously long.

This is the one of the most amazing moments of my life. Other than giving birth to the two terrors who are safely at home with Brenda.

Time goes so quickly and then it is my category. Angelina Jolie is announcing it. I hope I bloody win just so I get to meet her.

I do not expect them to call my name for a second, but they do. I sit there, stunned. William pushes me out of my chair and I walk up to the stage. I am standing in front of every actor I have idolised my entire life and standing with an actress I have always been obsessed with. Angelina kisses me on the cheek and says congratulations as she hands me the Oscar. My Oscar.

'I would like to thank the Academy for this honour. I cannot believe I'm here. This is every little girl's dream. I want to thank Jeremy, the director and Elizabeth, the writer, her script was perfect. What a role. Thank you to my fellow actors; Colin, Jennifer and Lucy. You guys were amazing.' The music starts, they want me to wrap up. 'I very quickly want to thank my amazing husband. You are my north star. I could not live without you. To my children,

Joseph and Amelia, and my best friend Claudia. Thank you, and thank you to everyone I forgot.'

Steven Spielberg. Steven fucking Spielberg walks on to the stage as I walk off and says congratulations to me. I almost faint.

I walk to a room full of journalists and photographers. I answer their questions and have a million pictures taken. Eventually, I make my way back to my seat.

'Wow, that was amazing! Well done, darling.'

'Yeah, well done, Tash. You looked really good. Like you belong.'

When the Oscars finish, we head to the Vanity Fair party. We meet up with Scarlet there.

'You didn't thank me during your speech, darling. Honestly, I'm so upset.' Scarlet tells me. I am not sure if she is joking or not.

'Oh, I'm sorry. I was just nervous, I forgot loads of people.'

'You didn't look nervous. You came across perfectly.' I know this is supposed to be a compliment but it comes across as an accusation when Scarlet says it.

'Anyway, let's celebrate. I won an Oscar!'

'Yes! Let's.'

Scarlet looks at the Oscar the way a hungry tiger would look at an antelope.

'Can I hold it?'

'Yes, of course.' I hand it over to her, reluctantly. I do not want anyone else to hold my Oscar.

'*Ew*, Scar, I can see Roman Polanski. Why the hell did they allow him in here? It's disgusting.'

Scarlet scans the room for him. She hands me back the Oscar.

'I am going to go and say hello.'

'Are you kidding?'

'No. Jeez, Tash, he's an artist. He makes masterpieces. Pull yourself together.'

I'm about to get into an argument with her but she's gone before I can. I swear to God, that woman has no morals. Having no morals is the quickest way to the top in Hollywood. I cannot believe she is not a world-famous superstar by now.

I spent the rest of the evening talking to famous people, dancing until my feet hurt and hanging out with two of my favourite people in the entire world. I will remember this day for the rest of my life.

# Chapter 31

## Now

I do not set my alarm for the next day. If the reviews are bad, they are not worth getting up for and if they are good then they can wait. Either way, I need to care less. The skill of not caring whether or not someone likes you takes a lifetime to master.

I can hear the motions of the house in action. The children are watching television and I can hear William in the kitchen. My morning sickness during my first trimester was trying and has carried on to the second. I lie there for a moment and let out a groan. I forgot how awful it is to make a baby. The second trimester is the best one too, the third one is going to suck. *Jeez,* why did I think it was a good idea to do this again! I hear the door go and I open my eyes.

It's William. He has a tray which has a full English Breakfast, tea and the papers on it. What a star.

'So?' I ask him. I need to know which way it has gone.

William pauses dramatically. Why oh, why does he have to pick up actor traits?

'They love you, darling. It's a resounding success.'

I sit up like a bolt.

'Really? They loved it?'

'Nothing but praise. The phone has been ringing all day There are even more flowers downstairs. I'm starting to worry that the flower shops will empty.'

I cry with pure relief. It worked. I am back. They love me again.

William places the tray on my lap and I pick up the fork. Then he lays out each paper at the relevant page.

'I will cut all of these out and place them in a book. You need reminders of how amazing you are. Next time people come at you just remember your long and illustrious career.'

I am bowled over with his love right now. He is the perfect husband. My ride or die partner. I love him beyond words. He kisses me on the forehead.

'Enjoy your breakfast. I'm going to clean the kitchen.' Damn, just when I thought he could not get more sexy. William heads down the stairs and I look at the reviews. They are all good. There is not one bad one. They say I am a powerhouse and the actress of her generation. I only hope the film studio bosses and directors are reading these reviews too.

I do not want to be back in front of the cameras when I am pregnant. Even though, I am barely showing I can see it in my face. So I produce another film. This one is a sexy crime thriller with a female lead. Yes, I would love to play the role myself but I will not. I need to spread the love around.

The streaming sites are really gaining ground now. The entire industry is changing so quickly it is breathtaking. Years ago, it was a terrible thing to be a television actor. The line between movie stars and television actors was a hard one. Never the twain shall meet. Now every film actor has done TV. They fight for the best roles. There is no line any more. Good work is good work.

I get a meeting with Netflix. I remember when Netflix was a company you rented DVDs from in the post. Christ, I really am old. Now they are a billion-pound company making some of the best film and TV shows. I want a piece of that action.

I dress up for the meeting in a Roksanda dress and Manolo Blahnik heels. I only hope they take me seriously, unlike Miles and Gyles. Twats that they are.

From the moment I walk in they treat me with respect and tell me they love my work. They offer me a multi-million-pound production deal. It took the new guard to give me the respect I deserve. I am elated. I start to think of all the amazing projects I am going to do. This is only the beginning.

When my driver drops me back home, Scarlet is on my doorstep. She is wearing a long, purple boho dress and Doc Martins. She has a wicker handbag and a long, string necklace with stones on the end. She looks like a mixture between a fortune teller and a homeless person. She has dyed her hair a bright red. I cannot believe Alex ever fucked this woman. I note that Bear is not with her. He never is. Maybe he is of school age now? I can never remember.

'Thank you, Martin,' I tell the driver, slipping him a fifty. He smiles and nods, then heads off.

'Hi, Scar.'

'Hey, Tash.'

We both just stand there. I do not want to invite her into the house. I know I will, of course. I have an inbreed politeness that I truly hate. But I will not make it easy.

'Can I come in?'

'Of course.'

I walk up the stairs and she follows me. I note that there is no coyness, no hesitation. I doubt she thinks she has done anything wrong.

I unlock the door and step through.

'Where are the kids?'

'At school.'

'Ah, yes, of course.'

'Where's Bear?'

'With my mother-in-law. She likes having him.'

'Grandmothers generally do.'

I take off my shoes and I head into the kitchen. Scarlet does not take off her boots. I think about asking her to but I don't want to appear uptight. She always thinks I am.

'Nice shoes. Manolo's?'

'Thanks,' I say, but I don't tell her whether or not she is right.

There is another awkward silence.

'Can I get you anything? Tea, coffee?'

'Do you have any herbal tea?'

Of course she wants herbal tea. I look in the cupboards.

'There is some peppermint.'

'Great, that will do.'

I boil the kettle and take out two mugs. I put a teabag in each. I can see Scarlet scrutinising me as she does. It makes me uncomfortable.

'You look,' she stops, trying to place it. 'Different.'

I don't want Scarlet to know I am pregnant. I know for a fact she has sold stories about me to the press.

'I've just been relaxing a bit, eating burgers, letting it all hang out, as it were. I've been behind the camera a lot.'

She nods. I think she bought it.

'I was sorry to miss you on your opening night.'

'Yeah, I'm sorry about that. Thank you for the flowers though, I loved them.'

'Claudia said you went for a really nice meal afterwards. You were always good at making the most out of life, celebrating whenever you can.'

'I guess I am.'

I pour the tea and hand it to her. She takes it and then places it on the table quickly. It's still hot, of course.

'Sorry, I should have placed it on the counter.'

'No, it's fine.'

'What can I do for you, Scarlet?'

She looks at me, hurt in her eyes.

'Can a friend not just drop by?'

I take time to think, twisting the ring on my wedding finger, which always calms me.

'Scarlet, I know you sold stories about me.'

'Oh, Tash. It's just a game. I never told them anything personal or horrible. I was doing you a favour, helping your career. I have always had your best interests at heart. Do you not remember when we were at drama school? I gave you so much good advice. I set you on your path. I have always been there, helping you out. I am like a manager or something.'

I do not like where this is going. No one takes credit for my career other than me.

'Calling me fat and telling me to lose my accent is hardly gold-standard stuff.'

'It gave you an edge.'

'Being in shape and doing accents are the basics of acting, Scarlet. You don't even need to go to drama school for that.'

I see a flash of anger. I don't know what she expects from this, but she is definitely not getting whatever it is.

She lets out a long, dramatic sigh.

'Don't be this person, Natasha.'

'And what person would that be, Scarlet?'

'The ungrateful bitch one.'

Relationships. They turn on a dime.

'Scarlet, I'm not going to just stand here and be insulted. You already did that once and I promised I would never allow it again. I'm not a punching bag for other people and their bullshit.'

'Everything was just given to you. Everything was easy for you. You never even worked for it.'

'That sounds an awful like that article that derailed my career, Scarlet. Almost word for word. Do you not find that strange? Quite the coincidence.'

I have hit the mark, I know it. It is so obvious now. I cannot believe I didn't see it. She doesn't say anything. She is unsure of her next move.

'It's not like that.'

'Then what was it like? Why did you sell out your friend?'

'We've hardly been friends. You dropped me quickly. You have never done anything for me. You are a selfish bitch.'

'What are you talking about? We have hung out loads. We FaceTimed and emailed even when you were in a different country. Then you just fuck me over. For what? Did you get paid?'

She looks away. I have always wondered how Scarlet survives. I know she doesn't get enough acting work to pay the bills. Well, until her divorce from Alex. I am sure that helped a lot.

'You're not a nice person, Natasha. You never have been. You're a stupid, skinny, entitled blonde. The industry just likes you because of how attractive you are. You're everything that is wrong with this industry. We need good actors doing good work, not Barbie dolls.'

'I'm what is wrong with this industry? At least, I did not sleep my way to the top. You fucked everything that moved! Funny thing is, it didn't even get you halfway up. Have you ever made a movie with your clothes on? Just wondering.'

Her rage is pure. I can see that she hates me. She throws her tea at me. It is hot enough to sting. I wipe it off my face.

'Well, that was mature. You can get the fuck out of my house now.'

'This is not your house. It's a fucking rental.' She throws the mug at me. I duck and it breaks behind me. The shards of ceramic go everywhere.

'Get the fuck out now before I call the police! I am not joking.' I take my phone and dial nine one one. I show her I am about to press the call button. She huffs, slamming every door on her way out. A drama queen until the end.

I walk to get the dustpan and shovel and I stand on a particular sharp bit of ceramic. It cuts my foot. I grimace and lift my foot, assessing the damage. It is not too bad. I step carefully to safety and wipe the cut with an antiseptic wipe and put a plaster on it. I place my hand on my stomach. That was scary as hell and I am worried all of the yelling and aggression hurt the baby. I had no idea Scarlet had such a vicious side. The betrayal stings. I hop to the sofa and lie down. A sadness is creeping at me. I have known Scarlet for half my life. I thought we would know each other when we were old ladies, that our children would grow up together. Now she is just another broken promise. Another shattered dream.

# Chapter 32

## Now

I wish I could see Scarlet's face when the news of my Netflix deal breaks. She will be so pissed off. She can take her mediocre career, her failed marriage, and her child with a trendy name and shove it all up her ass.

It is funny how much it energises you, having an enemy. The first two weeks after Scarlet's visit I was swept over by a depression so suffocating I thought it might drown me. William told me I was mourning my friend. We grieve when relationships end. It is only natural. I guess that is true. The end of things hurt, even bad things. I blocked Scarlet from my fake identity Facebook, my email, my phone, my Twitter and my Instagram. I have probably forgotten something. I tell Claudia what happens but she refuses to take sides. That upsets me. Maybe it shouldn't. But my experiences in life have taught me that anything less than complete loyalty has to be met with wary suspicion.

The pregnancy is kicking my ass. I was so young when I had my other ones. Being pregnant in your forties is a really extreme form of exhaustion. I do not even want to think about pushing this thing out.

I get a WhatsApp message from Claudia.

*Can I talk to you right now?*

*Of course*, I reply.

She calls immediately.

*'Oh, Tash,'* she says and immediately starts to cry.

*'Claud, what is it?'* I hate to hear her cry. She is not a crier, it must be really bad for her to be this upset. I let her cry some more to get it out. I worry about Helena – it must be her mother, or her father, something.

*'It's Geoff.'*

Oh, shit! That is not what I expected.

'And my mother.'

I am really worried now.

'Oh, hun, please tell me what's wrong.'

'Geoff has been screwing the nanny and my mother says I am being too middle-class about it! She says I should just go and have an affair too. She called me pedestrian. 'Men do what they do, darling.' I mean, what year are we living in?'

*'Geoff is the one who is pedestrian. I mean, the nanny? How much more of a cliché can you be?'*

*'She has massive tits. I mean, she could take someone out with them.'*

I try not to laugh but fail. Thankfully, Claudia laughs too.

'I think I'm going to slash his tires.'

'Well, take my advice, Carrie Underwood him. Do more than one tire – maybe all four. Geoff comes across as an organised guy and I'm sure he keeps a spare in the boot.'

Claudia laughs again.

'I feel better talking to you. You always make me feel so much better.'

'If William had sex with someone else, I would cut his cock off and shove it down his throat.'

'I have a weak stomach. I don't like blood.'

We take a moment to be happy in each other's company, even though thousands of miles separate us. A thought comes to me.

'Why don't you come here?'

'What, with the twins?'

'Yes.'

'That might be a nice break.'

'No, I mean permanently. Move in with us. Fuck him and your mother. We have space.'

'What about William?'

'He knows that when he married me you came with the package.'

'I am coming. I cannot wait. Thank you, you always save my life.'

'I'm here for you. I can't wait to see you.'

'Thanks Tash, you are always there for me. You are the best friend anyone could ever wish for.'

I hang up the phone. Claudia is coming with the twins to live with us. I am so excited.

I am tentative when I mention it to William. 'That's fine, darling. I always knew this day would come.'

I love how easy-going William is. He tends to take everything in his stride. He has become a bit of a dude since he quit his job. He wears his pyjamas most days and when he does dress, he wears jeans and a T-shirt. He goes on long walks and loves exploring New York. He has learnt a lot about the city and I love finding out what he has learnt.

He is a great dad and a loving husband. He reads all my scripts and still cooks the most amazing food.

'Unemployment suits you.'

He looks at me and smiles.

'Come over here,' he says and pats his lap. I go and sit on him. He puts his arms around me and kisses me. We go forehead to forehead. I love these moments, they power me. He feels like home. I want to stay here forever.

'I hated being a lawyer. I mean, I know I was the most liked kind of lawyer, but I still hated it.'

'Really?' I am taken aback. I never knew this. We have been together for over seventeen years and I hadn't noticed he hated his job. I am an awful wife.

'I didn't notice you hated your job. I feel terrible.'

'Well don't. I did my best to hide it well. I didn't want you to know.'

'Why didn't you tell me before?'

'What was I going to do? Tell my amazing, beautiful, ambitious girlfriend that I wanted to quit my job? I didn't know what I wanted to do with my life. I just took the easy path. I respect you so much. You had a dream and you went for it, but not everyone knows what they want in life. Some of us just meander along and never know what we are supposed to be. I guess not everyone has a purpose in life.'

'You should have told me.'

'When we were first together your income was erratic. Then I thought you would not be attracted to me if I was a house husband. I know you're not obsessed with status but the outside world is. I didn't want to be your loser husband.'

I stroke his hair as he talks. His hair is still a warm, chocolate brown. There is not one grey hair in it. I inhale his smell. I have been so wrapped up in myself I neglected him.

'Well, you're not a loser. And if you were a woman, you could quit your job and stay home with your children and no one would bat an eyelid. Why should it be different for you? I was reluctant when you mentioned quitting your job because I thought I was the reason you were doing it and you would resent me, or be unfulfilled. We don't need the money so I want you to do whatever you want. Even if that is living.'

He nuzzles the tip of my nose with his.

'Thank you. I think now is the time for new beginnings.'

'It is.'

We stay there for a while. Just enjoying the moment. Enjoying each other. The only thing that takes away from the moment is a ping from my phone.

'You should look, it might be the kids.'

I groan and take the phone out of my pocket. It is a news alert about me. Scarlet. I could kill her.

'It's a news alert saying I'm pregnant.'

'How did that get out?'

'How do you think?'

He rolls his eyes. 'Scarlet. That woman is the herpes of friendship. The gift that keeps on giving.'

I feel rage inside of me. Why can she not leave me alone and live her own life? I will never understand vengeful, bitter people. Sure, I have a list. But I don't go out of my way to ruin the life of the people on it. I just avoid them.

'I can see I am going to have to do something to take your mind off this,' William says, laying me down on the sofa and pulling my dress over my head.

'Well, hello, nice underwear. Should I be worried?' He gives me a cheeky eyebrow raise. I usually wear M&S underwear. The ones you get in packs. It never matches. Occasionally I have wondered if I should try harder.

'Victoria's Secret has a sale on. I thought "why not?" I wanted to feel put together for the meeting that I had. It is a happy fluke I am wearing them today.'

'Well, I approve of you letting me know your secret but I will have to remove them.' He undoes my bra with expertise and pulls down my knickers. He slips his fingers into my pussy. I groan with pleasure.

'Wow, you are unbelievably wet.'

'Of course I am, you're gorgeous. I need you to fuck me, now.'

He does not need to be told twice. He takes off his trousers and underwear and is inside me within minutes. He fucks me perfectly, not too hard, not too soft. This is the pleasure of marriage; someone knowing what you like. Having someone know every inch of your body and how to make it respond. Always having someone there to have sex with when you want it. Intimacy is the most precious thing in the world and not easy to come by. You have to grasp it with both hands when it comes to you.

Sex with William is perfect. Almost everything with William is perfect. Sure, he leaves his socks everywhere and he is messy, but as your relationships goes on you realise that these things are small and you are not perfect either. There are few things I find more enjoyable than being made love to by my husband. We stay in each other's arms after we climax, our nakedness bonding us.

'I always thought at some point you would leave me for a movie star. One of those ones that kill loads of people in their films and has muscles on top of muscles.'

'I always thought you would leave me for a younger and hotter woman.'

William lifts his head up and looks at me. 'There is no woman hotter than you. There may be ones that are younger, but you never need to worry about that. There is only you. There has only ever been you.'

'You are my only too. I love you now and forever. There is no action hero who could ever whisk me away.'

We settle into each other, knowing that the love we have is our greatest privilege of all.

# Chapter 33

## Now

The vastness of Central Park never fails to astound me. You see it so many times in movies so when you are actually walking through it yourself it feels surreal. My children have been watching endless re-runs of Friends. Every time they see New York in a film or television show, which is a lot, they get excited.

I want to spend every weekend with them. Sometimes they have other ideas. I barely see them due to my Broadway run. That is why I hate doing theatre. The run will end soon and my work, life balance will resume.

'Mum! Oh my God, look it's Zoe Gold!'

Amelia is pointing and getting very excited, indeed. I see a girl who looks eighteen at most. The children do not tend to get starstruck. They have had famous people around them from birth. They have been privileged from their first breath and it is my greatest achievement.

'Is she an actress?' Amelia does not usually get excited about actors. The children think what Mummy does it stupid and embarrassing. Amelia rolls her eyes. 'Of course, not, Mummy, and you should say "actor", otherwise it's sexist.'

Sometimes, I forget how brutal children are, but then I am swiftly reminded.

'My bad.'

This gets another eye roll.

'Don't say "my bad", Mummy, you're too old for that.'

*Ouch.*

'So not an…' I stop myself from saying the illicit, sexist word. 'Actor?'

'No, Mum, she is a TikTok superstar. She's so amazing. She has thirty million followers.'

'Even I know who she is, Mum. Everyone does. Social media, YouTube is the way forward. No one really cares about old media any more.'

'What is old media?'

'Television, newspapers, magazines.'

*'Ah!'* I think about what my children have just said. 'What about the cinema?'

'I think that will always exist because it's about the experience,' Joseph says.

'Good. I think it would be sad if the cinema didn't exist.'

Amelia has been watching Zoe Gold this entire time. Zoe has been taking selfies of herself. She puts the stick away in her bag. I hate those sticks; I think they are narcissistic and make the people who use them look like twats. But, then, I am old.

'I'm making my move,' Amelia says, heading towards Zoe.

'I'm going to go too,' says Joseph, clearly trying to be nonchalant about it.

Zoe Gold has her game face on. She clearly knows how to interact with her fans. She gives Amelia a huge hug and then Joseph as well. She takes selfies with each of them individually and then one of them all together. She is bright and bubbly. Her energy is off the scale. I think about my forty-something self. I feel permanently exhausted and I am not sure that it is just because of the pregnancy. I unconsciously touch my stomach, check on the little one. I have been wearing loose clothes as much as possible. Big bags have been my friend. We did not deny the pregnancy but we will not confirm it at all. The media think if you ever let them into your personal life then that is a pact and you are never allowed back out. Like the mafia. Screw 'em. I am not playing that game any more.

I watch the new generation and I think that I need to up my game and make some changes. It is a new world and I have stayed in the old one. I see Amelia point to me and then Zoe's jaw hits the floor. Holy shit. Does she know who I am?

She is coming towards me now. Zoe is dressed all in white. A white boho dress with long sleeves and ruffle detail, white denim jacket and white converse. She does not look real. Her skin looks airbrushed. She is wearing a lot of make-up but it somehow does not look trashy. I understand why Amelia is dazzled by this young lady; she clearly has the *je ne sais quoi*.

'Oh my God! I cannot believe it. You are Natasha Jones. I love you! Your work is amazing. I have seen everything you have ever done. You're my ultimate role model. Can we take a selfie?' I wonder if she is from New York, her accent sounds very valley girl.

I can see Amelia and Joseph behind her, their mouths open so much they look like The Scream.

'Of course. I would be honoured.'

Zoe takes the stick out of her bag and attaches her iPhone to it. She then lifts it and we both smile for the camera. She looks at the picture.

'It's perfect. Should we get one with your kids?'

'That would be great.'

Amelia and Joseph rush over and we all get our picture taken. Zoe looks at the picture with the eye of someone with very high standards.

'This one looks perfect too. It's so rare to get it right on the first try.'

'Great, thank you.'

'I will put them on my Insta. I cannot believe I met you. My fans will go wild. Could you come on my show? I would be so happy.'

Amelia squeals with delight and I can see Joseph doing a thumbs up.

'That would be great.'

'Wow! This has turned into the most perfect day.' Zoe goes into her pocket and hands me her business card. I take it.

'I'll contact you. We'll fix something up.'

'Great.' Zoe stands there for a moment, slightly swaying on her feet, then she pretty much launches herself at me and gives me a hug. I hug her back. She seems like such a sweet kid.

'Bye, see you soon.'

'Bye, have a great day, Zoe.'

Amelia stares after her as she leaves, girl crushing on her all the way. The rules of entertainment changed and I did not even notice.

We get ice cream in the park and watch the swans. These moments are always wonderful but sometimes they are tainted with sadness. They are so far away from my childhood. Poverty never leaves you. Your feet never feel firm on the ground. There is never a moment when you do not know that everything could be taken away from you and you will end up right where you started. That is the fear that never leaves.

# Chapter 34

## Then

I look through the clothes. They all look old, but some look older than others. A lot of them have pilling on them. I mean, they are okay, but they will all be a bit too big. None of them will be "me". I feel poor. I always feel poor. The kids at school know I am poor and they let me know it.

I am the girl on free school meals which, I once noted to my mother in an argument when she was pointing out how well my generation had it compared to her childhood, is the governments criteria for a child who is growing up in poverty. I only get new clothes once a year, when we get a voucher to buy me new school clothes. It is not much money and we buy my clothes from Woolworths. They are always shiny and full of static. I hate them. The feel of them on my skin mocks me.

When I went to school yesterday, all the rich kids had weird tan lines where their skiing goggles had been. They never talk to me. Even with the humiliation of a huge, white mark around their eyes, highlighted by their deep, brown tan. They always think they are better than me. Even when they look like a racoon in reverse. I hate them just as much as they hate me. Their lives are easy.

I wonder what it must be like; to be born into security and have no idea what the world is really like. Maybe they will find out one day.

Last night was a new low. Our electricity meter ran out. The only food we had in the house was potatoes. We ate them raw with a little bit of salt, y'know, for flavouring.

The rich kids who ski do not know what raw potatoes taste like. They never will.

I never knew we lived on the rough side of our town until one of my friends mentioned it. The shame burnt at me. It wasn't that bad, I thought. But the truth was I just did not know anything else. Little kids do not know they are poor. They need some bitch to point it out to them. Then they know how small they are.

I pick up the first item. A velvet shirt in a dark purple colour. It is okay. Not exactly fashionable. The next is a long, sleeveless dress with a zebra pattern. There are black trousers that cost more than the ones I have to wear to school, but they have pilling on them. There are also jeans and various jumpers and stuff. I look at this pile of hand-me-downs and I promise myself that as soon as I can I will buy my own clothes. They will be expensive, good-quality clothes, and I will never wear clothes that anyone else has worn again.

*London; nine years later*

My fingers feel as if they do not belong to me. The man is tall and looks down on me, sneering. I feel small standing in front of him and not just physically. I can't tear this ticker; there is no give. I get more flustered. It never occurred to me to practice something so basic. Finally, it gives and the stub comes away. The tall, older man with the white hair and sneering face does not hide his feelings.

'See, that wasn't that hard, was it?' he said condescendingly, taking pleasure in his cruelty.

He is dressed in a suit and looks like a professional. I wonder what happened to him in life to make him such a bastard.

I want to punch him. I really want to punch him.

I read about this job on an acting website. I say 'job' but I am volunteering at one of the most prestigious and famous theatres in the UK, hell, maybe even the world. They get millions in funding but here I am, working for nothing. I hide the bitterness; it will not get me far.

In return for my work, I will be given free acting workshops and I can see the shows for free. I can put the workshops on my CV, so I do it. I may even get spotted. This must give me a head start over other actors.

It takes an enormous amount of effort to not tell Mr Stuck Up to go fuck himself but instead I put on my best fake smile and I tell him, 'Have a good evening, sir. I hope you enjoy the show.' He slithers off into the darkness.

I take a quick look at the price of the next ticket that I tear; twenty-four pounds. There are hundreds of people here. I feel exploited. They could pay us, they just don't think we are worth the money.

I stay out of a British sense of politeness and, because I do not want the hours, I have already put in to be pointless. I want my reward.

The last ticket is torn. All the volunteers quietly enter the theatre and sit at the back. The show is not fun. It is dreary and depressing. The kind of theatre that bores you to hell but gets tons of awards. I hate depressing entertainment. Why tell the audience that life is hard and full of pain? They already know.

The actors are amazing, however. I learn so much just from watching them. When it finishes, I exchange looks with a fellow volunteer. He is a great older guy with a twinkle in his eye. His accent is Australian. He said he has done "boring things" to pay his way and now wanted to work in the theatre because there was 'more to life than money.'

'Well, that was heavy,' he says.

'No shit,' I reply.

'Well, who doesn't want to watch some murder, suicide and infanticide of an evening.'

I laugh. This guy is funny.

We get a filthy look from one of the other volunteers. This one is a hardcore bitch with a superiority complex. She has either been here for ages and thinks she owns the place, or she is related to someone here. We stop giggling and sit up straight for ma'am. To our horror she comes towards us.

'Can you go out and add some branding as the investors move to the champagne reception, thanks.'

All the volunteers are wearing black trousers and a white T-shirt with the name of the theatre on it. I start thinking there might be come free champagne going but I think better about getting my hopes up. Mrs Bitchface does not seem the generous type. I note that Bitchface never does any work herself. She just saunters around telling everyone else what to do.

I watch the investors as they walk by and I resist the urge to trip up the ticket twat. I wonder if they liked the show or they are just pretending so some gritty art will wash away their corporate souls. After they have all walked in, I follow them and walk around, wondering what to do now.

I can see the woman who runs the theatre clock me. She does not look happy and leans into Bitchface's ear and says something to her. Bitchface comes towards me. She does not look happy.

'What are you doing here? Keep away from the patrons, we don't want volunteers at the party. Stay in the back.'

Maybe if she had asked me nicely, I would have thought about it but I respect myself too much.

That is it. I will not take any more of this abuse. I smile and say, 'of course.' But inside, I know I will never be back. I cannot respect people who are so snobby and awful.

I had the last laugh as I still received the volunteer newsletter. I sign up for an acting workshop which is run by the two leads from the great but depressing play of various -cides.

I still hope that the people who run the theatre will be nice, or at least nicer. I need to have faith in my own kind. I still feel crappy about the volunteering and how horrible everyone was.

I arrived at the theatre with a packed lunch and was glad to see that a few people I knew were there. I put down my stuff and waved and smiled at the people I knew. The actors were split into groups and I was not paired with anyone I knew.

We warm up after we had been split into groups. I recognised them from RADA. There was a lot of mirroring and trust exercises. Then we took our personal items from our bags and got into a big circle. We all discussed what we had and what it said about us. This was followed by some improvisation and then we act out a scene each. I could feel my happiness rising. This is why I act. Because it makes me happy. When you are actually in that zone, telling stories, there is no other feeling like it.

I get singled out for a scene which I do with the lead actors from the play. I am in my element; I give the scene my all and show what I can do. By the end of the scene, I am crying and so are the two leads. I swell with pride. The male lead turned to the rest of the class.

'Wow, did you see that! That is real acting. That is how you do a scene. Let's all give Natasha a round of applause.'

I knew that I would remember this moment, and the kindness of these actors who were already successful and so much more talented than me. I looked at the sea of faces clapping with mixed emotions, some happy and genuine, others jealous. It is perfect, no matter. I am happy and people I respect have told me I am talented. Nothing is going to rain on my parade.

*Now*

My vagina is on fire. You block out how bad labour is but you never forget, no, what you forget is what your vagina feels like after your baby's massive head comes out of it and it takes them an hour to stitch you back up. At first, I would pee by pouring a jug of hot water over myself while I did. I have given up on that now and I just pee in the shower. I do not even care how disgusting it is. I earned the right when I gave birth. I haven't peed in the bath. So, there is that. Not yet anyway.

We announce the birth the way of the new celebrity; an Instagram post.

It is a black and white picture that does not really show her face. I have just given birth and I am wearing minimal make-up. Of course, minimal make-up for an actress means foundation, pale brown eye shadow, a bit of eye liner, brown mascara and nude lipstick. Done by myself, not a make-up artist. My hair is okay but not its usual fabulous. I decided against doing a full Kate Middleton. My image has to be more real. As we take the pictures, write the caption, and publish the post I feel dirty. Like I am violating my own life. I have enough self-awareness to know that I never miss an opportunity. I am on 24/7.

We made sure the face is not visible. That way they cannot call us hypocrites. They would not leave me alone during my pregnancy. It was so crappy. Every time I went to a store, I was on the cover of a magazine looking like a whale. I have no idea why I thought I could hide it. I look the post over.

*Our hearts are full of love. Our daughter, Eloise, entered the world today. She is perfect in every single way. Thank you for all your support, from our family to yours. Xxx*

It is fine. I do not want to hire a social media manager. I want it to come across as genuine because I want to be genuine. I also cannot afford any more staff. The children are in private school and our outgoings are still huge. Now we have a new baby. The general public have no idea how much it costs to run a movie star. I have been doing theatre for six months and trying to produce films that I believe in. The money is not exactly rolling in.

I look down at Eloise as she suckles at my breast. I breastfeed all of my children. I wanted to give them the best start and it has the bonus of being great for weight loss.

William is asleep next to me now. We just watched a documentary on the oxycontin drug problem. I get that it was supposed to be a cautionary tale but one of the people in it was talking about how they were in a car accident and as soon as they took the drug, they felt nothing, no pain at all. I am still in agony from the birth and that is the kind of numbness I need in my life right now. *I wonder if it works on emotional pain. Oh, ha ha,* I think to myself.

I never thought I would get to a point where I would not miss acting. I have been fuelled by my ambition my entire life. Now I am excited to stay at home with my baby. I was forced back to work too soon after having my children. I want to do it properly this time. I can be a good actress and a good mother. I will find a way.

Three weeks after the baby is born, I find out Scarlet is suing me for a share in my production company. She says we started it together and I owe her years of money and profit. There is no low that woman will not sink too. William immediately starts to deal with it. She seems to have forgotten that I am married to a lawyer. William tells me not to worry. She has never actually done any work for the production company and when I finally got around to registering it for VAT and stuff it was only my name on all the paperwork.

Even Claudia did not want to deal with the nitty gritty business stuff. Claudia only came to act occasionally and Scarlet only reared her head for a role when the hard work was all done. It is all over the papers and magazines, of course. This whole thing is probably just a publicity stunt on her behalf. She wants to gather sympathy. People like her are obsessed with being victims. I will push the thing out of my mind. She is trying to ruin this special time for me. I will not let her. I am going to tell William to countersue just to let her know not to fuck with me. That bitch needs taking down.

Claudia arrived with the twins this morning. Pretty much at the same time, I got served. That was uncomfortable. I gave Claudia a look, I could not help it. If she lives here, she cannot still be friends with that woman. I need discretion and loyalty. Claudia and the nanny have been dealing with the twins and unpacking.

The time alone to decompress is much needed. I put some coffee on and I do my deep breathing.

This baby is an easy baby. 'Trick babies' my mother calls them because they give you the false sense that this is easy and then you end up having another one. I am pretty certain Eloise was my last egg but I would be up for it. I have always loved babies and family. I would give up my entire career for my children if I really had to.

'Gosh, darling, how did you manage that?'

I look at Claudia. Being a woman scorned suits her. She had been losing too much weight, drinking too much and had taken to wearing dowdy tweed and unflattering denim. From what I could see on Facetime anyway.

'I am sorry about this stuff with Scar, darling. It is so tough on you.'

I roll my eyes at the nickname being used.

'You don't need to be sorry. You didn't do anything. It's all that hippy bitch.'

Claudia does a grimace. 'Isn't that a bit strong?'

I give her a look that shows her what 'strong' really is.

'Okay, okay. I know. She has gone too far but I think she is just doing it for attention. You know she is like a little child.'

'Does that make it okay?' I ask as measured as I can.

Claudia is taken aback at my fury but I do not care. She is making me look bad in the press. Again. She cannot stop taking her bitterness out on me. This lawsuit will be the last thing she takes, the last time she hurts me. There will be no excuses and no forgiveness.

'No, of course not.' Claudia finally responds. She knows I am serious now, I can tell.

'Can I get you a coffee?' I ask her, drawing a line under that bitch and her latest wrath.

'You do know that I know I was never a part of it. We had that conversation in the beginning but you did all the work and Scarlet and I both fucked off. It was all you, I know that. You have always been generous. She is the one in the wrong. Everyone will know that.'

Claudia's words mean so much to me that I go over and hug her. She hugs me back. It is a beautiful hug full of love. It makes me happy.

'That coffee would be great. We have a lot to catch up on.'

'Do you need a nap?'

Claudia laughs.

'You know me so well.'

'I do indeed.'

'I will have the coffee and then nap for twenty minutes. It's a good alarm clock.'

I hand Claudia her coffee. She is typing on her phone so I place the cup on the counter in front of her.

'Sorry, just sending a quick text.'

'That's okay. I hope it's to that bastard Geoff letting him know you are living it up in New York.

'Ha. Pretty much.'

Claudia puts the phone down and we have our coffees together. It's amazing having her with me again, instead of driving around the English countryside being some twat's housewife.

'That is good coffee.'

'Damn right it is. The Americans have great stuff.'

Claudia nods to concede.

'Right, I am going up to bed. I will be a better conversationalist when I have had a nap.'

'Have a good sleep, Claud.'

'Thanks, darling.'

She heads upstairs. As she goes, I notice she has left her phone on the counter. I pick it up to give it to her but then decide against it. Then I see the message on the phone.

*Claudia, please. Do not choose Natasha over me. It is not my fault. Please call me. Please. Scar, Xxxx.*

Then I get that warm feeling all over again.

# Chapter 35

Sometimes all the stars align. Now is one of those times. Scarlet dropped her claim not long after Claudia's message. So, I countersued. I settled for an apology and a declaration that she had nothing to do with my production company. The victory sits with me for weeks, making me unattractively smug. I don't even care.

I watch as the children run around the desert. The nannies have a lot of work cut out for them. The next shot is being set up and I watch as a journalist from Empire interviews me. I brace myself for the usual 'female director' question. I look over at the journalist. She is a pretty redhead. She looks young, maybe twenty-five.

'Your films are so inclusive. They call you the feminist film director. What do you think about that?'

The question makes me think. I like that. The journalist is smiling, she knows it was a good question. One hopes she is not just buttering me up.

'What a great question. Well, I don't want to think about being inclusive. I just want it to be standard. We have great childcare on set. If you have a young family, we will accommodate you. We want actors to know that. Childcare is important. I have a great relationship with a lot of great women, but also a great relationship with men. I want this to be the last wave of feminism. I want the hero of the story to be female and no one notices and no one feels a need to point it out. The day it's not a thing is the day we win.'

The journalist looks happy with that answer.

'You seem to have had some trouble getting certain projects off the ground. Do you think it's harder for a woman to get funding?'

'Well, I think female film directors' – I cringe when I call myself that, I wish we did not need our gender pointed out, just like men don't – 'are held to a different standard. Also, we get that bullshit statement that "female films do not sell" which is rubbish. Look at the Marvel movies, look at Bridesmaids. That point has been disproven again and again. Now we have Netflix and all the streaming sites.

When I first started, there was a lot of sexism in the industry. There were powerful men abusing their power and few roles for women. The roles were generally terrible and were just girlfriend parts, which changed into mother parts and then grandmother. The industry has changed but not fast enough. We still have a long way to go but change is happening.'

'That's great, thanks.'

The interview has wrapped up.

'Please feel free to stay as long as you want. You can interview anyone else too.'

The journalist's face brightens. 'I would love to, thank you.'

I walk down to the scene. I look through the lens and I check the shot. I take a moment. Breathe it in. Claudia is there, getting into character. So are Patricia and Alex. I cannot believe William suggested it, but we decided to go into business together. He is a producer now. We love working together. I never thought we would do well spending so much time together. The kids even work on the set, though I hope neither of them wants to be an actor. I am happy. Life turned out better than I ever thought it would.

I yell, 'Action!' – on the first scene from Girl on the Wire. It starts.

Natasha Jones becomes the change, she wants to see in the film industry.

*Actress Natasha Jones has become a producer and director because she did not like the roles she was getting. Now she is the voice of a generation and is making Hollywood more inclusive from the inside out. This follows a period where the actor was the laughing stock of the industry and was thought of as nothing more than another mediocre blonde.*

*The resurgence began with a show on Broadway that was met with widespread critical acclaim. Next up came a series of films that she produced and then an Emmy award-winning television show. Natasha took a back seat as she had a baby at forty-one and made a move from London to New York. There was a brief moment of discontent as she fell out with old friend Scarlet Walsh, who sued her for a part of her production company, but Natasha won the legal battle.*

*A Netflix deal worth hundreds of millions was signed and since then Natasha has been unstoppable. As a triple-*

*threat performer, director and producer, she took a sexist and abusive industry and then made it on her own terms. Who knows what is next for this working-class girl done good. She is now richer than her wildest dreams and has turned into a one-woman film industry. Watch this space.*

I read the latest piece on myself and I feel, finally, that I have made it. Even if I am not a star one day. Even if I am no longer an actor, I have made a change in this industry that will last even when I am gone. I hope there will be others like me who keep fighting the good fight.

I walk into the garden and they are all there. Claudia and the twins, William, Joseph, Amelia and Eloise. It is a tiny little world, the ones you truly love and trust, but when it comes down to it, they are not that small after all. They are all the love and happiness in the world. The anchor in life's ocean. You make your own world and you fight for it. Fundamentally, there is nothing else because there does not need to be.

They cheer when they see the tray.

'I love mojitos!' Claudia says, a little too merrily.

'I thought you were on a health kick?' I ask her.

'Oh please, that lasted for a second. I'm a single mother of twins. I deserve liquor.'

'I hear you, sister. These kids wear you out.'

'*Jeez,* thanks, Mum.' Amelia screws up her nose. Maybe one day she will find out herself.

Claudia comes and takes a drink and so does William. The children take theirs. They are virgin ones in their special cups but they do not need to know that. I place my drink down and lay the tray against the table. It is full of the most delicious food; hummus, cheeses, roast vegetables, deli meat. There is cake in the kitchen ready to come out. The champagne is in the sink, cooling down in some ice. We are not celebrating for any one reason. Life is enough of a celebration. You need to find the joy and happiness where you can and make the most out of every single day.

I close my eyes and take a huge breath in, hold it, and let it out. Satisfaction. That is what this is. I know there are more tough times ahead. There always are, but it's okay. I am made of a mixture of steel and Teflon by now. Bring it on. Bring it all on.

William's lips on my forehead make me open my eyes. We smile at each other. We have been together for almost twenty years. An achievement in any light but add in Hollywood? It is a huge deal. Time goes faster when you are famous. Opportunity is everywhere. At least it looks like an opportunity. Things are not better just because they are new. You need to hang in there and fight for what you have got.

The children take their drinks and head down to the bottom of the garden where there is a ping pong table. I watch them as they go. They are so grown up now. It seems like only yesterday they were babies. Now they are both taller than me.

'You make a mean cocktail.'

'I do indeed, Claud.'

William takes a sip. 'Yeah, it's one of your many talents.' He gives me a wink.

'Oh, honestly guys. If you are still going to love each other after all of this time, can you at least have the common decency to not find each other attractive? It's not fair on everyone else.'

William and I both laugh. Eloise stirs in William's arms but quickly goes back to sleep.

'Sorry, Claud. It's gross, I know.' I tell her. 'How did your date with that musician go anyway?'

'Really good. We fucked three times.'

I put my face in my hands. William almost drops Eloise. Then I laugh.

'Well, I always say the easiest way to get over a man is to get under another.'

'Hey, you,' William tells me. I try to look sheepish.

'Trouble is, men don't wait until the last relationship is finished.'

'Hey, you,' William tells Claudia this time. Poor guy. He is outnumbered. I see Joseph and Amelia coming towards us.

'Heads up, behave. We don't want the children to know we do all of the stuff we tell them not to,' I say.

'Mum, you will never believe this. Amelia just told me what she wants to do with her life. I think you are going to love it.'

I get excited immediately. We have been discussing career options with the children for a while now. We want to help them get on their paths.

'Mum, I want to be an actress! Just like you,' Amelia says.

'And, Mum, I want to act too,' Joseph adds.

300

I look at my children and no words come out. There are only the ones in my head; oh, no.